Abruptly, without quite knowing how it happened, she found herself across the marquess's lap. She barely had time to look up into his laughing eyes before he murmured, "You know me so well," and his lips came down on hers.

Verity had never been kissed before. The touch of the marquess's lips on her mouth set her body aflame. All at once her rules flew out the window, and she could not get enough of his warm, firm lips. She returned his kiss with reckless abandon, shutting out any emotions save the ones he was calling forth. . . .

By Rosemary Stevens
Published by Fawcett Books:

A CRIME OF MANNERS
MISS PYMBROKE'S RULES

MISS PYMBROKE'S RULES

Rosemary Stevens

FAWCETT CREST • NEW YORK

A Fawcett Crest Book
Published by Ballantine Books
Copyright © 1997 by Rosemary Stevens

All rights reserved under International and Pan-American Copyright Conventions. Published in the United States by Ballantine Books, a division of Random House, Inc., New York, and simultaneously in Canada by Random House of Canada Limited, Toronto.

http://www.randomhouse.com

Library of Congress Catalog Card Number: 96-97166

ISBN 0-449-22518-6

Manufactured in the United States of America

First Edition: March 1997

10   9   8   7   6   5   4   3   2   1

With love for my family—
J.T., Rachel, and Tommy

and

For Cynthia, Russ, Melissa, and Linda

Dear Reader,

Two of my favorite things are the Regency era of British history and cats! So, it was only natural for me to combine them for my series, *The Cats of Mayfair.*

I hope you enjoyed reading about the adventures of Knight in Masked Armour last May in *A Crime of Manners.* Please rest assured that Knight has grown even rounder than when we last saw him. You remember how Colonel Colchester keeps him content by supplying culinary delights. And speaking of being happy, I have it on the best authority that Giles and Henrietta are still deeply in love and are expecting their first child.

In this book, please meet another Mayfair cat, Empress. Unlike Knight, Empress is careful to maintain her svelte figure, although she does indulge in a dish of cream now and then. She gets a lot of exercise bringing together Perry and Verity in *Miss Pymbroke's Rules*—and ends up drinking something stronger than cream!

Please do look for *Lord and Master* (on sale in early November 1997). I'll be introducing you to Mihos, a cat who is being paraded around Astley's Royal Amphitheatre billed as the world's smallest tiger! Daphne and Anthony rescue him only to become embroiled in an intrigue involving their growing feelings for each other, a stolen Egyptian treasure, and Anthony's unique manservant.

I love to hear from my readers. Please write to me at P.O. Box 951325, Lake Mary, FL 32795-1325. Kindly enclose a SASE if you wish a reply.

Rosemary Stevens

Chapter One

"I make it a rule never to fancy myself in love," Miss Verity Pymbroke stated matter-of-factly in response to Lady Iris's odious suggestion that she marry. With unshakable composure, she raised her cup to her lips and took a sip of hot tea.

Seated next to each other on a dark blue satin settee opposite Verity were two older ladies, immediately recognizable as sisters, though their appearances differed greatly.

Lady Iris was dressed in the fashion popular in her youth, complete with powdered white wig, white paint, highly rouged cheeks, and a small black patch by the corner of her lined mouth. Other than this eccentricity, Lady Iris was a pattern of practicality compared with her sister, Lady Hyacinth.

That lady, often concerned overmuch with her health, sat wrapped in a mound of heavy shawls, which served as protection against an imaginary chill in the room. She appeared much shocked at her young friend's proclamation. "Verity, dear, how can you say such a thing? The gentlemen are so attractive. We females are helpless against their appeal and cannot resist falling in love with them. Why, I recall many occasions in the past where my genteel upbringing battled with my lustful passion for the gentlemen. The lure of love always prevailed, I assure you."

Embarrassed by this bold assertion, Verity nevertheless found herself suppressing a smile. She suspected Lady Hyacinth's amorous adventures were products solely of the lady's imagination, but kept her own counsel on the subject out of respect for her kindly, if fanciful, neighbor.

Had Verity believed for a moment Lady Hyacinth's past had been one-tenth so lascivious as the lady declared, she would have been deeply appalled.

"I have yet to meet a gentleman who could sway me from my convictions of what is proper behavior for a lady," Verity responded piously.

Lady Hyacinth absently raised a hand to her head and patted a red curl of a hue unknown to nature. "I confess I cannot understand you, dear child. Furthermore, it appears to me that what Iris has suggested is the only possible solution to your difficulties. There is no way other than marriage for a lady of good birth to be comfortable in the world, unless she has financial independence, which you do not."

Unable to remain silent any longer, Lady Iris rapped her cane on the floor, causing the teacups on the table to rattle ominously. She barked, "Ye gods, Verity, I said you should marry, not fall in love. And as for pretending the two go together, I say stuff and nonsense! Don't let Hyacinth put her wishful notions in your sensible head. I was married for thirty years, and I tell you I doubt I saw my husband above twice a twelve-month. It was an arrangement that suited us both. Can't even remember his face, now that he's been buried, tombed, and grassed over these eighteen years past."

Turning her head to glare at her sister, Lady Iris continued with the outspokenness admired in her generation. "What do you know of marriage, Hyacinth? I take leave to point out you've never been married, and you're perfectly content, ain't you?"

Lady Hyacinth promptly clasped her hands to her ample bosom in a gesture of distress, her wrinkled face a picture of anguish. Her sister's thoughtless reminder that she remained a spinster at the rather advanced age of two and sixty was like a knife wound to her romantical heart.

Gasping for breath, Lady Hyacinth managed to utter, "Oh, I am having palpitations. Merciful heavens, how cruel you are, Iris."

Alarmed, Verity set her teacup down and rushed to Lady Hyacinth's side. She reached over and picked up a vinaigrette from a small table next to the settee and offered it to the older woman. "Oh, please, calm yourself. I know your sister did not mean to hurt your feelings."

At this statement, Lady Hyacinth made a sudden, remarkable recovery and glowered round Verity at Lady Iris. Her voice took on a superior tone when she said, "You know I could have married anytime I pleased, Iris, but I could not settle on just one gentleman. And now that my health is so uncertain and I must remain here . . . well, I daresay it suits you since you desire company and the only gentleman who ever looked at you was that fusty old man you married because no one else would have you."

"Damn your eyes!" Lady Iris shouted, raising her cane above her head as if to strike her sister.

Lady Hyacinth, having successfully goaded her and knowing full well Lady Iris would never harm her, assumed a triumphant expression at her sister's display of anger.

"Ladies!" Verity exclaimed. She edged her way to sit between the two women on the settee and grasped a hand of each—one plump and one thin. "Do I need to remind you of the importance of a harmonious relationship among one's family members?"

Lady Iris rolled her eyes.

Lady Hyacinth sighed with resignation.

Both sensed one of Verity's high-minded sermons on "Treating One Another As You Wish To Be Treated Yourself" coming on. They knew once Verity got started on what she considered to be her "moral duty," little could stop her.

Verity stood up and turned to face the ladies. She threw back her head in a noble posture and lectured. "Each of you needs the other above anyone in this world. You must value your connection and not allow petty feelings of jealousy or competition to loosen family bonds. How I miss my own dear sister, Louisa."

Distracted momentarily from her purpose, Verity's gaze turned toward the sunlight shining in through the tall windows of the drawing room. Her voice took on a wistful tone. "I have written Louisa several letters begging her to come home from Portugal. Her heart must yearn for the consolation that only a sister could give her during her time of grief."

Lady Iris seized the opportunity of Verity's digression to return the conversation to her young friend's plight. "It's been two years now since Louisa lost her husband in the war, and she still hasn't torn herself away from all those soldiers to see how you fared. Not even when your mother, God rest her soul, passed away last spring. Verity, you've got to stop thinking Louisa will come home and share your financial difficulties."

"Yes, Verity dear," Lady Hyacinth said with something like a sniff. "Take it from one who *knows*. Having to rely upon a sister for one's bread can be lowering for a delicate constitution."

Lady Iris scowled at Lady Hyacinth. "Hmph. It hasn't kept you from eating Cook's scones. And as for your stomach being fragile, I say fustian. I never knew anyone who could pack away the food—"

Lady Hyacinth interrupted her, saying hotly, "If you knew anything at all about *current* fashions, Iris, you'd know the Regent himself prefers plump ladies."

Verity experienced a moment's worry that the sisters were working themselves up to another quarrel.

But Lady Iris refused to give her sister the satisfaction of reacting to her taunt and instead directed her attention to Verity. "If you do not contemplate marriage, then according to the intelligence your man of business imparted this morning, you will shortly be under the hatches."

Verity could not repress a shudder at the truth of these words. She sighed heavily. Although he did not stir any tender feelings in her, there was one man she might marry.

If only her friend, Mr. Cecil Sedgewick, would propose, she mused. She could easily envision a life spent with that worthy gentleman.

They would devote their days to good works. Evenings would be spent quietly conversing by the fire. They would be content to grow old together, and Verity need never fear the life her mother had endured married to a despicable rake. A life that had broken that lady's heart, bringing on a decline that eventually led to her death last year.

Alas, Mr. Sedgewick had never mentioned marriage. No doubt his mind was far above it. He devoted his time to expounding on moral purity hoping to impress the bishop, for he earnestly wished the bishop would award him a position.

Picking up her reticule, Verity spoke in a low voice, "Yes, you are right, my lady. If you will excuse me, I must go home. I shall work in my rose garden and try to think of a way out of my difficulties."

Lady Iris had been watching the play of expressions across the young girl's face. She rose to place her veined hand on Verity's arm. "Stay a moment, gel. I have another idea."

Lady Hyacinth stood as well, and she and Verity looked at Lady Iris expectantly.

Lady Iris took a deep breath and began. "I've thought of a plan that will benefit us all. I have heard how difficult it is to lease a house for the Season, especially now when it's already March. And a house at a desirable address, which South Audley Street most certainly is, would fetch a prodigious sum. Verity, you must hire your townhouse out for the Season. You may come and live with Hyacinth and me."

Lady Iris saw the protest rising to Verity's lips, and she squeezed the girl's arm gently. "Wait, before you say a word. I know your rule about accepting charity, but pray, listen a moment."

Cleverly, Lady Iris appealed to Verity's righteous nature. "You will be helping us, as well as yourself, because we shall expect you to pay us a small amount for living here. And Miss Woolcott may return to the country as she has wished to do this age."

Verity's brows had drawn together in consternation at Lady Iris's scheme, but at the mention of a way she could not only help her two friends, but could please her old governess too, her countenance lightened. "It may answer."

Lady Hyacinth gasped aloud. "Oh, do say yes, dear Verity. While it is most pleasant having you reside next door, why, to be in the same house shall be the coziest thing imaginable. Besides, think of the money you will have even after you pay us part of the leasing income. And I assure you that any sum you give us will be most welcome. Iris can be somewhat of a spendthrift, leaving me in doubt sometimes whether I shall be able to pay for my patent medicines. That awful man at the apothecary has refused me any further credit—"

"Enough, Hyacinth!" Lady Iris commanded her sister. Glancing sidelong at Verity, she said, "Naturally, if you feel you could not bring yourself to reside, even just for the Season, with two cantankerous old women like Hyacinth and me, we'll understand."

Verity gave each lady a quick hug. "Do not be ridiculous. I would adore staying with you. You must know how much I rely on your kindness and friendship."

Both older ladies beamed.

"But where will we find a respectable family to lease the house?" Verity asked doubtfully.

"You leave that to me," Lady Iris said, leading her to the front door. "We may not find a family but perhaps a lady and her companion, or even, er, a gentleman."

Verity whirled around from the door to state firmly, "I must make it a rule that whoever it is be of a virtuous mind."

"As you wish, Verity," Lady Iris said with unaccustomed meekness just before closing the door on her young friend.

"This is so exciting," Lady Hyacinth declared, rubbing her hands together. "I must go upstairs and decide on a bedchamber for Verity so the maids can begin airing it at once. You cannot know how devastating dust can be to one's respiratory system."

Lady Hyacinth trailed up the stairs in her bundle of shawls, leaving Lady Iris to return to the drawing room.

Out from under the settee a beautiful silver-gray cat emerged, blinking her slanted blue eyes at the increased light. Around the top of her head was a ring of pure white fur, giving the impression of a crown. She placed her front paws forward and indulged her fluffy, long-haired body in a good stretch.

"Well, Empress, she's agreed to my plan . . . or what she knows of it," Lady Iris said, arranging herself on the settee.

The cat wound sinuously against the lady's skirts.

Reaching for a saucer and the cream, Lady Iris poured a tiny amount of the rich liquid for the purring cat and placed it on the floor.

"Now all that needs to be done is to convince Carrisworth to move out of his house and into Verity's. A small task, indeed," Lady Iris stated, sarcasm lacing her gruff voice.

Having devoured the cream, Empress began the dainty task of washing. Licking her paw thoroughly, she used it to clean around her whisker pad.

"After that," Lady Iris said with a yawn, " 'twill be simple enough to bring the two around to my way of thinking. Verity needs someone like my cousin's grandson. A man who'll keep her from being so serious. And Carrisworth . . ."

Lady Iris leaned back to rest her bewigged head on the back of the settee and paused in her strategizing to consider his lordship. "Let us just say that many a rapscallion has been brought to mend his ways by the love of the right lady. Yes, the two will balance each other agreeably, Empress."

The cat paused in her ministrations to gaze at her mistress with an oddly thoughtful look.

"But how do I wrest Carrisworth from his home? 'Tis a puzzle," Lady Iris muttered before drifting off into a light sleep.

Empress slunk from the drawing room, apparently intent on finding an open window from which she could escape into the Mayfair streets.

Later that night over in Mount Street, Peregrine Rolf, the seventh Marquess of Carrisworth, was entertaining guests. The occasion was his thirtieth birthday. His townhouse overflowed with all manner of persons, whose greatest common interests appeared to be a love of strong drink and the pursuit of pleasure.

Damsels of the Fashionable Impure, fueled by free-flowing champagne, and scores of drunken young bucks evoked an atmosphere that would make a Cyprian's ball seem like a church meeting.

Although his neighbors were long used to his lordship's fondness for parties, even they had closed their windows and drawn their curtains against the raucous noise and indecent sights.

"By Jove, I would have wagered a monkey this was to be a quiet celebration, Perry," Sir Ramsey "Randy" Bertrand goaded his friend. "Perhaps a simple *party of three*."

Lord Carrisworth, rather the worse for copious draughts of champagne, lounged in a striped chair. He languidly raised his quizzing glass to study a passing female whose gown had fallen from her shoulders, leaving her charms blatantly displayed.

His lips spread in a devilish grin before he responded to Sir Ramsey's sally. "Have you been visiting the print shops in Bond Street, Randy?"

"No need to. The caricatures of you and the twins are all over town. You cannot be surprised. Even you have to admit putting Monique and Dominique under your protection was bound to set tongues running on wheels."

Lord Carrisworth raised one dark eyebrow. "Being a gentleman, I admit nothing."

"A gentleman? That's rich." Sir Ramsey let out a shout of laughter.

The marquess joined him in his mirth. But what Perry was really not admitting, not even to Randy, was the exact nature of his relationship with the twins.

Monique and Dominique had taken the theater by storm one month earlier upon their arrival from France. Seventeen-year-old identical twins with golden blonde hair, cornflower blue eyes, and luscious figures, their innocence had immediately captured the interest of Lord Armstrong and Lord Davenport, aging lechers with large purses. The two lords had argued loudly at the clubs as to which gentleman would have which of the chits.

Listening in disgust, Perry had not been able to bear the thought of the young girls being used by the smelly old rogues. In a show of altruism that shocked even himself, he had promptly made them *both* a very generous offer, which was quickly accepted, and established them in a house in Half Moon Street.

He then sat back to savor the resulting outrage amongst the ton. What he had not done was anything more than keep up the pretense that they were his mistresses by escorting the girls to the Park or the Opera, considering them to be no more than tiresome children.

Sir Ramsey tossed off another glass of champagne. "Where are the fair charmers this evening?"

Waving a manicured hand in a careless gesture, Carrisworth replied, "I have given my servants the night off, so I shall no doubt call upon the twins later to, er, help me out of this tight-fitting coat."

More masculine laughter followed this pronouncement.

Neither gentleman noticed when the silver-gray cat hurried past the entryway of the drawing room.

Empress slipped into the deserted kitchens. No tantalizing smells were in the air. No cook was bustling about, ready to stop her work for a moment to hand the pretty kitty a treat.

The cat made her way over to where the scullery maid usually slept on a straw mat in the corner. The girl's absence left Empress without anyone to pull a string or an old ribbon across the floor in a much-loved game of chase.

Her whiskers turned down, Empress left the kitchen to stalk off into a deserted anteroom. A single branch of candles, placed on a table by the window, provided a soft glow of light. The cat crossed the room and hopped up onto the table. Placing one dainty foot in front of the other, she padded across the smooth wood surface.

Unfortunately for the marquess, the branch of candles was placed perilously close to the edge near the draperies. A flick of the cat's tail sent it to the floor.

It took mere minutes for the flames to spread.

At the first cries of "Fire!" the Marquess of Carrisworth instantly sobered. His shouted instructions for everyone not to panic went unheeded as people scrambled for the stairs leading to the hall.

"Help me get everyone out, Randy! I shall look for anyone upstairs," Carrisworth called to his friend and barely waited to see if the man was capable of complying with the request.

He had to push his way into the hall. On the landing he grabbed a young man and ordered, "Have the watch notify the Sun Fire Company."

Hoping furiously his man of business had paid the premiums so the fire company would not let his house burn to the ground, he turned and raced up the stairs. Thick smoke blanketed the hallway and burned his lungs with each breath he drew.

He found three amorous couples secluded in bedchambers and alerted them to the peril. Shepherding them downstairs, he noted grimly that the drawing room he had vacated minutes before was engulfed in flames.

Out on the street a crowd had gathered. "Harkee, even the Quality has their troubles," a voice said in the darkness.

With relief he saw the men from the fire company had arrived and were working to control the blaze. Thankfully, everyone had escaped unharmed.

Lord Carrisworth worked alongside the firemen until at last the fire was out. While he had been struggling with the flames, he had not been able to assimilate the damage done. Now, he entered what was left of the hall and looked with a mixture of shock and horror at the charred black walls. The once magnificent mahogany table, whose polished surface had always held a bowl of fresh flowers, was reduced to a pile of ashes at his feet.

"Ain't safe in here, your worship," a man's voice warned. "You're Lord Carrisworth, ain't you?"

Staring at what was left of his family townhouse, the marquess nodded. "What of the upstairs?"

The fireman shook his soot-blackened face sadly. "I'm sorry, milord." He wiped his brow with a dirty handkerchief. "You've got yerself a pretty mess, but the house'll hold up. I'd figger on six months o' work, though, to put it back to rights. Can't tell you how many fires I've put out that got started by an overturned candle."

Carrisworth's gaze swung to the man's face. "An overturned candle?"

"That's what it were, milord. An accident, to be sure." Tugging at his forelock, he prepared to take his leave. "Well, you won't be needing us any more this night."

After the man left, Lord Carrisworth went outside to stand on the stone steps. The crowd had dissipated. He spotted one of his footmen walking with a halting step toward him.

"My lord! What 'appened?"

"As you can see, my townhouse has been heavily damaged by fire. When the other servants return, board everything up. Exercise caution, though, I do not want anyone injured. When the house is secure, everyone is to go to Duxbury House. I shall bring you back to Town after the repairs have been made."

The footman was young and unsure of himself in front of his master. Shifting his weight from one foot to the other, he asked, "My lord, when you say, er, *everyone* is to go to the country, do you mean even Mr. Wetherall?"

A long-suffering sigh escaped the marquess's lips. "Devil take it! No, I am sure I do not. Tell Wetherall I shall engage a room at Grillon's, and he may meet me there. I daresay he will deliver me a rare trimming for this night's work."

The footman bowed his way back down the steps and hurried around to the rear of the house.

Carrisworth remained where he was. What a birthday celebration, he reflected wryly. For a moment, he closed his eyes and thought of the paintings of his father and mother and of his ancestors, which hung upstairs. What had become of them? Not that he cared a snap of his fingers for the portrait of his mother. But the others . . . probably burned beyond repair, he decided with a twinge of self-disgust.

The watch called out the hour—three o'clock. The night was clear and crisp. The stars shone down as if their brilliance was just for Mayfair.

Suddenly, a plaintive wail sounded from the direction of the marquess's feet. "Miaoooow."

His lordship opened his eyes, looked down, and swore roundly. Then, he recognized the cat. "Good God, Empress, is that you?"

"Miaow!"

"What are you doing wandering around outside at this hour?" He bent down and picked up the animal. Examining the paw Empress had been favoring, Carrisworth muttered, "Lady Iris will have my head if you have hurt yourself during this cursed fire."

At the marquess's touch, the cat gazed at him innocently with wide blue eyes and began purring.

Unmindful of the picture he presented, his lordship cradled Empress in his arms and started down the steps. Dispensing with the use of a coach, he walked in an easterly direction, turning left when he reached South Audley Street.

The cat shifted position in his arms, causing a shower of hairs to land on his lordship's coat. Lord Carrisworth spared a moment imagining Wetherall's reaction when the valet found cat hairs clinging to what was now his master's only coat.

But, there was nothing for it. Lady Iris's pet must be returned to her at once. The marquess knew his grandmother's dear cousin often spent wakeful nights, and he did not want her to discover Empress missing at this hour.

Lady Iris was indeed awake when the marquess arrived on her doorstep. Not wishing to disturb the butler, she answered the door herself. "Carrisworth! Empress! Here's a pretty kick-up!"

She swung open the heavy door, her gaze taking in the marquess's disheveled appearance. Soot stains marred his fine burgundy-colored coat, and his cravat appeared grayish. A streak of black ran across his jaw. Even in all his dirt, though, Lady Iris thought him wickedly handsome and wished, not for the first time, she was considerably younger and totally unrelated to the marquess.

Transferring the cat to Lady Iris's outstretched arms, Carrisworth bowed low. "Lady Iris, I am afraid injury befell this unfortunate creature at my townhouse. Examine her left front paw, if you please."

Lady Iris grasped Empress's paw and gave it a cursory glance. "Seems fine. What the devil happened?"

"It pains me to say it but my townhouse nearly burned down this evening. An overturned candle, I am told. Luckily, no one was hurt. I was entertaining—it was my birthday, you see."

"An overturned candle," Lady Iris muttered weakly. She shot a disbelieving look at the cat in her arms.

Empress met her gaze for a guilty moment, then struggled out of her mistress's arms and scampered away in the direction of the kitchen.

"Surely, nothing so dramatic was necessary," Lady Iris shouted after her. Then she turned back to the marquess, who gazed at her quizzically.

The older lady pulled a woolen shawl tighter about her shoulders and said briskly, "You must stay the night with

Hyacinth and me, Carrisworth. I'll call a maid to make up a room."

The marquess stayed her with a hand. "My lady, I would not put you to the trouble. Besides, I have left orders for my man to meet me at Grillon's."

"I forbid it," Lady Iris declared. "I'll send a footman with a message for your servant to join you here. You are family and will remain where you are. I've a perfectly good bed upstairs."

Lord Carrisworth's eyes twinkled merrily. "Lady Iris," he drawled with mock severity. "You shock me."

"Oh, cut line, you naughty boy," she reprimanded, pleased with him. "Come along up to the drawing room. Bingwood will bring you a glass of port while your room's being prepared."

The marquess was too weary to make any further protests and allowed Lady Iris to shepherd him upstairs. It wasn't every day one lost one's home and turned thirty in the bargain.

In addition, he'd remembered Grillon's was terrifyingly respectable. He shuddered at the thought of lodging there.

Yawning, he decided he was better off staying with a couple of kind, old eccentrics. What could possibly happen here?

The next morning dawned sunny, but cold. The Marquess of Carrisworth awoke at ten, his unshaven face pressed down on an unfamiliar lacy pillow. The events of the previous evening came rushing back, and he permitted himself a groan.

"Just so, my lord," Mr. Wetherall agreed in frosty accents. He stood by the door, his sparse, elderly frame rigid with censure.

Please, God, Carrisworth prayed, not a scold before breakfast. He unwound his naked body from the bed. Nightclothes were abhorrent to him.

Adopting a cheerful manner while the valet helped him into a dressing gown, he said, "I trust you were comfortable last night, Wetherall. I shall have a shave and go downstairs to thank our hostess. Then we shall see about arranging someone to put the townhouse to rights."

Mr. Wetherall produced the shaving supplies, and after the marquess was seated, meticulously began his task. "May I inquire if we shall be sending for Weston before you venture out, my lord? I have brushed your only coat, ridding it of all the animal hair that somehow found its way onto the surface, but if you would permit me to say so, its condition is not in keeping with your lordship's customary elegance."

All this was said while the valet's left eye twitched convulsively. The marquess knew this signal of disapproval from long experience.

The Marquess of Carrisworth was not a man to tolerate insolence from his servants. In fact, he could be quite demanding. It was, therefore, ironic that the oldest family retainer, the one he could not dream of pensioning off, would be most prone to speaking his mind to his master.

The valet paused in his work, holding the razor at what the marquess thought was a menacing angle. "Also, if I may be so bold as to remind your lordship, all of *my* clothes were ruined in the fire as well."

Lord Carrisworth waved a hand impassively. "Naturally, you will have whatever you require. If you are finished, I should like to dress and go downstairs."

Mr. Wetherall lowered the razor, but his eye twitched alarmingly. "My lord, perhaps a tray sent up to your bedchamber until a new coat has been procured—"

"Oh, I am not so stiffly on my stiffs with the Ladies Iris and Hyacinth. Family, you know."

Thus, some minutes later, the marquess was in the dining room clad in the reprehensible coat and pantaloons from the evening before, helping himself to a generous portion of kidneys, ham, toast, and eggs.

Lady Iris was the only other person at the table. Lady Hyacinth never left her bed before noon.

Wise enough to wait until his lordship had put away a large portion of his breakfast, Lady Iris at last deemed it time to march forward with her plans. "How long do you guess 'twill be before you can inhabit your house, Carrisworth?" she asked in a deceptively casual tone.

The marquess took a sip of coffee before replying. "The man from the Sun Fire Company estimated several months."

"As bad as that, eh?"

"Yes. But you may be at your ease, I shan't impose on you that long, Lady Iris. I shall look for lodgings or maybe a house—"

A large crocodile smile creased Lady Iris's face, making the star-shaped patch she wore by her mouth rise halfway up her cheek. "Upon my honor! Nothing was ever more providential. The lady next door finds herself in straitened circumstances and wishes to let her house. 'Twill be the very thing. I'll just fetch my shawl and we'll call on her immediately before she—that is, before the house gets away."

Lord Carrisworth had no opportunity to form a reply before Lady Iris abruptly picked up her cane and left the room. He helped himself to a rasher of bacon and wondered idly what maggot the lady had taken into her head.

* * *

Walking up the steps of the townhouse next door, his lordship felt decidedly sour on the idea of living in such close proximity to Lady Iris.

His previous meetings with his grandmother's cousin had been brief and infrequent. Now, he saw she showed an alarming tendency toward being a managing female.

He avoided the type assiduously. He could just imagine her reaction to his choice of friends—male and female—not to mention his parties. And, leasing a house directly from what he assumed would be another aged lady fallen on hard times, one who would make all sorts of stipulations to their agreement, was not a pleasant thought.

Some excuse for not taking the house would have to be found.

The butler who answered the door informed Lady Iris and the marquess that Miss Pymbroke was working in her garden and escorted them through a prettily furnished morning room. Opening the glass doors that led to a walled garden, he bowed and withdrew.

Lord Carrisworth saw a female dressed in a service-able gray gown bending over to retrieve a basket brimming with freshly cut roses. A worn chip-straw bonnet hung down her back on a black ribbon.

She stood up slowly, turned around, and faced her visitors.

The startled marquess drew in his breath sharply. "Manna from heaven," he murmured.

A single shaft of sunlight beamed down directly onto the lady's head, giving her a halo. Although her brown hair was ruthlessly scraped back into a severe knot, golden lights danced from its clean, shining surface. Her velvet brown eyes appeared huge in a delicate face notable for its perfect ivory complexion. A straight little nose and a beautifully shaped mouth, a mouth that his lordship thought positively begged for kisses, completed her angelic appearance.

Lord Carrisworth leaned against the doorframe, crossed one booted foot over the other, and smiled lazily. He would take the house . . . and the lady.

Chapter Two

Verity stared wordlessly at the tall stranger who stood framed in the doorway.

His eyes were a dark emerald green, the lids heavy and curved, giving him a languid, sensual look. Thick, glossy black hair fell in disarray over a broad forehead. The cut of his coat emphasized his wide shoulders and slim hips.

"Verity, may I present the Marquess of Carrisworth?" Lady Iris was saying.

For some reason, Verity felt breathless. The heady scent of the riotous rose bushes around her seemed almost too pungent. Her hands began shaking, and suddenly, she dropped the basket of roses.

The marquess bowed low and strolled with a nonchalant grace to Verity's side. He knelt at her feet and gathered the roses back into their holder.

Finishing his task, Carrisworth straightened to his impressive height. He held one red rose between them, and his long white fingers caressed the flower, while his eyes never left hers for an instant.

"Miss Pymbroke," he murmured, his deep voice causing her heart to leap, "you must take care. Something so lovely and fragile should be cherished by an expert hand."

The look in his eyes, the subtle message behind his

words, the meaning she could only guess at, snapped Verity out of her trance.

Her mind registered the fact he was inappropriately dressed in evening clothes. Upon closer inspection, she discovered the eyes she had been admiring were shot with red. His firm, full mouth was stretched in a decidedly wolfish grin.

Oh! Here, surely, was a rake of the first magnitude!

Everyone knew rakes spent hours practicing their art of seduction. Had not her body just been behaving in a most peculiar way? She congratulated herself for taking his measure so promptly.

Verity snatched the rose from Carrisworth's fingers and took a determined step backward. She placed the flower on top of the others in the basket. Her chin came up, as she said coolly, "Thank you for your assistance, sir."

He raised his dark eyebrows in what she interpreted as surprise at her icy response. There was a maddening hint of arrogant self-confidence about him. Why had Lady Iris brought the handsome viper into her garden?

Verity wrenched her gaze away quickly lest he somehow detect the effect he was having on her. Turning to Lady Iris, she spoke with a calmness she was far from feeling. "To what do I owe the pleasure of your company, my lady?"

Lady Iris looked at the young girl's flushed face and ignored the question. "Verity, your cheeks are pink from the sun. Come inside, gel, and offer us some tea."

Verity picked up the basket of roses. Good manners forced her past the marquess, whose face she noted held an expression of amusement. She led the party through the doors into the morning room, stripped off her gloves and tossed them, along with her bonnet, onto a nearby table where she placed the basket of flowers.

Across the room, a middle-aged woman appeared and sat in a chair. She pulled a tremendous amount of knitting out of a large bag and placed it in her lap before noticing the company. "Oh, Verity, I did not know we had guests," she bleated, her gaze darting nervously over his lordship.

"How are you this morning, Miss Woolcott?" Lady Iris inquired. "May I present my late cousin's grandson, the Marquess of Carrisworth?"

A relation! Heavens, Verity thought, looking with distaste at the shameful way the marquess was bending over Woolsey's weathered hand. Surely he would not be so brazen as to place a kiss upon it—it appeared he would. Woolsey simpered.

Verity pursed her lips in disapproval. She sat down on the gold satin sofa close to Woolsey's chair as if to protect her companion from the marquess.

Undaunted, Carrisworth had only a moment to wait while Lady Iris seated herself on the chair opposite the sofa, leaving the way clear for him to sit next to Verity. He looked at her, seemingly pleased with himself. "This is a comfortably furnished room," he drawled, with what Verity thought a strangely proprietary air.

"I find it so, my lord," she replied curtly. He would not be allowed to practice his flirtations in her house. She might have to endure his company during this unwanted morning call, but after that, since she never went about in Society, most likely they would not meet again.

A maid settled a heavy tray on the table in front of her. Trying to disguise her annoyance at the marquess in front of the others, Verity busied herself with the tea things.

But the marquess was not a man to be ignored. "You may want to consider ordering a fire made up, Miss Pymbroke. Is this room always so chilly?" he inquired blandly enough, but she saw the teasing twinkle in his eyes.

The teacups trembled in their saucers as she passed them to Lady Iris and to Woolsey. Preparing a cup for the marquess, she was suddenly seized with a mad desire to fling the contents into his lap. Mayhaps that would persuade him she was not one to fall into his arms. Verity gritted her teeth. The temerity of the man! He was persistent, she'd give him that.

Instead, passing him the cup with every evidence of martyred civility, it was she who almost received a drenching when Carrisworth sat forward abruptly and clasped her hand.

Startled, Verity's gaze flew to his face. The marquess adroitly removed the cup from her nerveless fingers, placing it aside and holding her hand firmly. He spared but a glance at the two older ladies, assuring himself they were busy examining Miss Woolcott's knitting, before raising a handkerchief to one of Verity's fingers.

"You must have pricked yourself on a thorn, Miss Pymbroke," he whispered.

Struck speechless, Verity watched in fascination as he wiped at a smear of blood. Appalled at the intimacy of his action, she tried to tug her hand away, but he held fast. "Let go of me at once, sirrah," she commanded, keeping her voice low.

His lordship did not oblige her. Instead, before she knew what he was about, he lowered his dark head to mere inches above her hand. She could feel a whisper of warm breath against her wounded finger. A tingling sensation ran through her blood while at the same time her stunned brain cried out in protest of his disgraceful behavior. He would not dare kiss *her* ungloved hand as he had Woolsey's!

As if reading her thoughts, the marquess met her gaze, and again Verity saw the teasing twinkle in his green eyes before his lordship slowly, reluctantly released her hand.

Lady Iris loudly cleared her throat.

In the wink of an eye, the Marquess of Carrisworth was sitting at his leisure, drinking his tea, as if he had not just made advances to a young lady of virtue in her own home.

"Have you explained to Verity why we have come this morning, Carrisworth?" Lady Iris asked.

The marquess placed his empty teacup on the table. "Yes, and I'm happy to report Miss Pymbroke has been all that is kind. She took pity on me when I told her my townhouse burned down last night."

Struggling to retain her equanimity, Verity listened to him with increasing astonishment.

Leaning back in his seat, the marquess smiled on the company and continued, "Being able to lease a suitable house from a gracious lady has made me feel the luckiest of gentlemen. All that we have left to decide is when I may move in." He turned to her, a look of unholy glee on his handsome face.

Still feeling the heat in her cheeks from the marquess's bold conduct with her hand, Verity felt a fresh rush of indignation at his latest piece of impudence. Lease *him* her house? She might as well rent the premises out to a raree show! Insufferable man, how dare he say she had agreed to such a scheme?

She opened her mouth to protest, but Miss Woolcott asked bemusedly, "What can this mean?"

Lady Iris hastily explained the plan to lease Verity's townhouse for the Season while Verity lived next door, ending with, "And, Miss Woolcott, you may at long last return to the country."

Miss Woolcott's knitting fell to the floor when she lurched from her chair to embrace Verity. "Oh, my girl, thank you! I know you will be as happy with the Ladies Iris and Hyacinth as I shall be with my widowed brother back in my dear village with its marvelous sheep and cows."

Verity returned the woman's hug while the marquess politely gathered the fallen knitting. Miss Woolcott thanked him and flew from the room declaring she must begin packing.

"How neatly this has fallen into place," Lady Iris said and beamed at the young people.

"Indeed," Verity responded crossly, feeling as if she had been manipulated and was trapped in an odious coil. Her conscience would not allow her to disappoint Woolsey. And, because rudeness was foreign to her nature, she shrank from insulting Lady Iris, who had been so kind since Mama's passing last year, by denying the lady's relation occupancy of a house she had previously agreed to lease.

It was all his fault, Verity decided, glaring at the marquess. He must know she would not want to lease the house to a rackety sort such as he. But, then, he would hardly spare a thought for her feelings, she reflected. Rakes never concerned themselves with the sensibilities of others. Her father certainly had not cared for his wife's or either of his daughters' feelings when he had run off with an actress.

The butler entered. "Mr. Cecil Sedgewick has called, miss. Shall I show him in here?"

Lady Iris moaned. "Must we?"

"Of course," Verity replied, frowning at Lady Iris.

Turning to the waiting servant, she said, "Yes, Digby, and please bring fresh tea."

The butler bowed and left the room.

The marquess rose to his feet, a glint of humor in his eyes. "I shan't keep you from your guest, Miss Pymbroke. Would three days be sufficient time for your removal next door? I would like to occupy the house by the end of the week."

Verity wished she might turn up her nose and send him away with a flea in his ear. However, since her finances were past praying for, such emotions would have to be kept in check. She must make it clear, though, that he follow certain rules if he were to live in her home.

Rising to her feet, she threw back her head in a martyred way and said, "Yes, three days will do, my lord, but we have the rules of your tenancy to discuss."

He waved a careless hand at her. "Rules? Miss Pymbroke, I rarely concern myself with such trivialities. My man of business will call upon you tomorrow and settle whatever sum you require for the arrangement."

Verity stood aghast at these proclamations.

Lady Iris struggled to her feet with the aid of her cane. Adjusting her high white wig she declared, "Good. Everything is decided."

In an aside Verity missed, Lady Iris added to the marquess, "Let us take our leave before I am forced into the company of that moralizing prig, Sedgewick."

Verity faced her soon-to-be tenant. "I was not speaking of money, Lord Carrisworth. What of the servants? Will you be bringing your own and thus turning mine out into the streets? If so, I take leave to remind you how difficult it is for servants to find a place."

The marquess raised a brow and gazed at her speculatively. "How unusual you are, in that you should consider the fate of mere servants. But, you need not bristle up that way, I have sent my servants to the country and have no intention of displacing yours."

Verity breathed a sigh of relief. "Very well. Now, the other matters to consider—"

At that moment, Digby opened the door to reveal a slight, thin man in his middle twenties dressed in black. His sandy-colored hair was noticeably thin on top, and he peered out at the world from behind a pair of spectacles that magnified his pale blue eyes. In his hands, he carried a sheaf of pamphlets.

He looked at the gathering with an air of perplexity. "Good day to you, Lady Iris. Miss Pymbroke, I hope I have not called at an inopportune time?"

Smiling sweetly at him, Verity hastily introduced Mr. Sedgewick to his lordship, noting with indignation how the marquess merely gave a fleeting nod at the aspiring cleric.

For his part, Mr. Sedgewick bowed and blushed beet red upon hearing the marquess's name.

Lady Iris begged leave to be excused, but Carrisworth lingered. He gazed down at Verity as his hand reached for hers. In a voice full of meaning, he murmured, "I shall be next door should you require assistance of any kind."

Verity's large brown eyes sparkled with anger.

Mr. Sedgewick coughed and turned away.

Carrisworth's thumb gently moved in circles across the back of Verity's hand, sending a rush of warmth up her arm. She pretended not to feel anything, positive this was another of his rakish accomplishments, and with what she thought was a brilliant air of unconcern, removed her hand from his and dropped him the briefest of curtsies.

He laughed aloud, startling her. "You know, Miss Pymbroke, when you purse your delectable lips that way, I find myself hard pressed to refrain from kissing them."

Wisely, he strolled from the room before Verity could form a response. She found she had been holding her breath and now released it in a long sigh. She stood for a moment, holding her hands to her warm cheeks. It was deeply disturbing, to one used to being in total command of her emotions at every moment, to find her feelings swung back and forth like a pendulum by none other than a careless pleasure-seeker. She resolved not to let him affect her so in the future. After all, toying with her feelings was but the merest game to him.

Mr. Sedgewick moved toward her from where he had retreated by the window and eyed her sternly. "Miss Pymbroke, I cannot imagine why a lady of your good sense would allow London's premier rake to cross her doorstep."

"London's premier rake? As bad as that?" Verity asked faintly, motioning the gentleman to a chair near the tea table. When they were seated and Mr. Sedgewick, having placed his pamphlets by his side, was fortified with a cup of tea, she continued. "I judged his character at once, of course. But, he is a relation of Lady Iris, and as such I could not but treat him courteously."

"I daresay many noble families have a black sheep," Mr. Sedgewick ventured. "It is most unlike Lady Iris, though, to foist unwanted company on you." His magnified eyes peered curiously over his teacup at Verity. "You appear agitated, Miss Pymbroke. Was there a purpose to his lordship's unpleasant visit?"

Verity quelled the notion that Cecil Sedgewick was like a ferret when it came to gossip. It was simply, she told herself, because of his desire to serve people that he concerned himself with their troubles. And she *had* landed herself in a bumblebath, agreeing to let her house to Lord Carrisworth. Not that she had precisely agreed. The sneaksby had tricked her into capitulating.

Placing her teacup carefully on the table, Verity folded her hands in her lap. She spoke with a quiet dignity that belied the emotional turmoil the marquess had caused. "I find myself in circumstances that require me to practice economy. The Ladies Iris and Hyacinth have opened their home to me, and I shall be renting out my house for the Season. Lady Iris brought his lordship here as he requires temporary lodging, and we reached an agreement. I shall remove next door presently."

Verity watched the growing astonishment on Mr. Sedgewick's face as she imparted this news. She wondered briefly if he would be brought up to scratch by the knowledge she had been reduced to leaving her home to gain an income, but these hopes were quickly dashed.

"By all that is holy, Miss Pymbroke, could you not have dissuaded him? Why, every feeling must be offended by a man of Carrisworth's reputation calling on you, no less to move in bag and baggage. Surely a respectable family would be more desirable tenants." Mr. Sedgewick's complexion had taken on a purplish hue, and he produced a handkerchief with which to mop his damp brow.

Though Verity's feelings on the matter ran in perfect harmony with Mr. Sedgewick's, she felt her temper rise. If he was so appalled by the plan, why not suggest an alternative? Why not offer her marriage?

None of these ruminations showed on her ivory countenance. Patiently, she explained, "As I have told you, his lordship is related to Lady Iris. It was my Christian duty to aid him. He is the victim of a fire, after all, and one must be charitable."

"A . . . a victim?" Mr. Sedgewick blustered. Then, his tone changed to one suitable for addressing a small child. "Miss Pymbroke, you are too good, too virtuous to realize . . . Lord Carrisworth's misfortune is the result of his own folly. The fire occurred during one of his parties, one of his *sinful* parties, and the vengeance of the Almighty was heaped justly upon him. It was in the *Times* this morning," he concluded with relish.

Verity's mind reeled from this latest proof of his lordship's rakish ways. "Oh! How very like one such as he, I imagine. But I fear there is naught I can do at this point save keep my distance from the marquess as much as possible. And that you may be sure I shall do, Mr. Sedgewick."

Though he tsk-tsked loud and long, Mr. Sedgewick seemed appeased by this statement. The remainder of their time together was spent going over the pamphlets he'd had printed for her special cause, and the two parted much in charity with each other.

After the distressing events of the morning, Verity perceived she would have to lie down upon her bed for an hour, so she might revive her spirits enough to undertake the task she had set for herself later that afternoon in Drury Lane. But after some fifteen frustrating minutes had passed, spent tossing and turning while the Marquess of Carrisworth's handsome features remained imprinted behind her closed eyes, Verity rang for a cold nuncheon and prepared for her outing.

Lounging at his ease backstage at Drury Lane's Theatre Royal, Lord Carrisworth, restored to his usual elegance in

Weston's finest blue superfine, allowed his former mistress, Roxanna Hollings, to massage his temples.

He had come to the theater to visit Monique and Dominique and interrupted a rehearsal. The stage manager had grudgingly allowed the company a respite, especially as it wouldn't do for him to antagonize a member of the nobility when he was trying to establish his newly rebuilt theater against the heavy competition of Covent Garden.

The twins had chattered away at Carrisworth until called by their dresser. As if on cue, Roxanna had swept to his side, her raven hair hanging loose to her waist.

The marquess was not suffering from the headache. But Roxanna, after hearing of the fire, had exclaimed he must be and offered one of her massages. As he was never one to turn away a pleasure, Carrisworth let her perform her ministrations.

Rather than standing behind his chair for this benevolent service, Roxanna leaned forward in front of the marquess so he might enjoy a perfect view of her luscious breasts, which rose tantalizingly from the bodice of a revealing crimson-colored gown.

"How does this feel, my darling Perry?" Roxanna cooed.

"Mmm . . . wonderful. You always have been artful with your hands," he replied with a grin.

Roxanna lowered her voice to a husky whisper. "Perhaps you are chastising yourself for casting me aside in favor of those two French trollops. I shall not hold it against you, my love. It was a mere whim on your part to shock and scandalize Society. Now that those print shop caricatures are all over Town, your purpose is served, and we may be comfortable again. Why not come to my house tonight after the performance? I have obtained some new scented oils. . . ."

The marquess fixed his gaze on her sapphire blue eyes. Roxanna Hollings was one of those females who always managed to project an air about her that bespoke a woman who favored a state of undress. Indeed, he'd spent many pleasant evenings with her that bore testimony to his theory.

When he'd first decided to rescue Monique and Dominique from Lord Armstrong and Lord Davenport, he'd sent a munificent diamond necklace to Roxanna to signal the end of their three-month relationship. Since then, he had frequented a certain house whose madam, a Mrs. Dantry, could always be counted on to provide him with a beauty who would eagerly satisfy his physical needs.

He raised a dark eyebrow at Roxanna. "My dear, what would Rupert say of such behavior?"

Her pink lips formed a pout at the mention of her new protector. She dropped her hands to her sides and straightened. "I don't care two straws for Rupert's opinion. You know that. In fact, you and I know each other very well, do we not, Perry?" She ran her hand down his lordship's muscular thigh.

The fact that she *did* know him so well was the problem, in the marquess's estimation. However tempted he might have been by her offer, he drew back at her astute judgment of at least part of his motivation when it came to the twins. He reveled in his reputation as a dissolute rake. It kept people at a comfortable distance.

And Roxanna had seen the truth.

He rose to his feet and, regretfully, ran a finger across the top of her white breasts. "As much as it pains me to refuse you, I have no wish to meet Rupert across a set of dueling pistols."

Removing his hand, he turned toward the doorway, missing the look of cold fury that passed over his former mistress's face.

Across the hallway in the Green Room an altercation seemed to be in progress. The marquess walked to the entrance and stopped short at the sight that met his eyes.

Clad in a Quakerish black wool gown, Miss Verity Pymbroke spoke earnestly to a small group of young actresses who were vehemently disagreeing with her. Each held a pamphlet in her hand like the one his soon-to-be landlady was reading from. By squinting his eyes the marquess could make out the title. *Evils of the Stage.*

His lips twisted in amusement.

"Not again!" Roxanna snapped, appearing at his elbow. "How monstrously boring. The girls and I have taken to calling that moralizing Methodist, Miss *Prim*broke."

The marquess made no comment to this witticism. Focusing his attention on Verity's huge pansy-brown eyes, her sweet countenance, and the lovely glint of gold in her hair, he decided she possessed an innocent appeal refreshing to his jaded gaze. As to the lady's personality, Carrisworth believed his initial vision of her as angelic had proven prophetic.

Studying her sincere expression, he realized Miss Pymbroke cared deeply about the subject she was expounding on. He wondered what could have caused her to feel it was her mission to try to reform actresses. Experience told him most of the women on the stage loved the life and basked in the attention given them. True, after a certain age many could no longer find protectors, but the wiser ones planned for this eventuality.

Miss Pymbroke lectured on, oblivious to his presence. "Young women are lured from their homes by the promise of fame and money, when the reality is that vulgar gentlemen use them for their own immoral pleasures—" She broke off here, her face flushed with embarrassment at the delicate nature of her words.

"Tell us about those pleasures, fair lady," a masculine voice taunted.

Carrisworth swung his gaze to the gentleman who was slowly making his way toward Miss Pymbroke. The man's red hair was cut in a fashionable Brutus crop, but because of its wiry nature, it looked more like a red squirrel's fur. That hair made him easily recognizable as James, Lord Davies. He emulated the Dandy set. His shirt points were ridiculously high, and the bright salmon color of his coat clashed violently with his hair.

Lord Davies was known to the marquess because of his acquaintance with Sir Ramsey. Randy had often referred to the baron as bad ton, and suspected the reckless gamester was not above the unforgivable practice of loading his dice or fuzzing his cards.

The baron moved close to Verity. "Tol rol, for all your Puritan airs, I'm persuaded a man with my wealth, title, and superior taste in clothing could persuade you to change your thinking." He snaked an arm around her waist, pulling her close.

Verity struggled against his strength. Pressing both of her palms firmly against his chest, she said, "I am not interested in your purse or your title. You are exactly the sort of man who preys on these young girls. Have you no conscience, sir?"

Several of the actresses sniggered.

Carrisworth shrugged off Roxanna's restraining hand

and advanced into the room swinging his quizzing glass to and fro on its black cord. His voice was deceptively casual. "Davies, is it not? I must say I am surprised to see you here. Thought I heard there was a wager at White's on the outcome of Brummell's opinion of Alvanley's new coat. I should not think you would miss it. Remove your hand from Miss Pymbroke, by the way."

Freed from the baron, Verity raised a shaking hand to her hair and secured a strand that had fallen loose. The appearance of the Marquess of Carrisworth in the Green Room unnerved her more than Lord Davies's advances. That gentleman's expression turned mulish, but only for the space of time it took him to perceive the iciness of the marquess's eyes. He reluctantly dropped his arm to his side, saying pettishly, "Just looking for a little fun, Carrisworth. You get your share."

"Indeed I do," the marquess agreed cordially, "but with *willing* females." Turning to Miss Pymbroke, he observed her expression turn from relief at her release to one of stubborn purpose.

Before she could attempt to return to her sermonizing, he said, "Miss Pymbroke, I am sorry to inform you that Miss Woolcott has overexerted herself in her efforts to be on her way out of London. She requires your assistance."

Verity gasped in alarm.

Ignoring the stricken look in her brown eyes, he concluded this Banbury tale with an offer to take her up in his carriage. "I assure you the conventions will be observed as I have my tiger with me, and I assume that Friday-faced chit outside the door is your maid. You have not already bespoken a vehicle, have you?"

"No, my lord, I came in a hack," she replied distractedly. Accepting his proffered arm, she called to the maid and allowed herself to be hurried away.

Watching their retreating backs, Roxanna's blue eyes narrowed.

Lord Davies assuaged his wounded pride by commencing to flirt with a buxom girl dressed in a shepherdess costume.

Outside in the street, Lord Carrisworth halted their progress and turned to face her. "I daresay you have never seen a play, am I correct, Miss Pymbroke?"

"Y-Yes, I mean no, I have not," she stammered, confused by the question. "Pray, sir, my companion's condition is not serious, is it?"

Dusk was falling over London. The streets were growing more crowded as people hurried home to prepare for the evening ahead.

Lord Carrisworth contemplated the young woman standing anxiously before him. She could not be more than eighteen, yet she had affected the manner and dress of an old prude. He experienced a sudden desire to see her dressed in finery, with her hair curled about her face in the latest fashion. "I shall tell you only after I have your solemn promise to attend the theater with me on an evening of my choice."

For a moment, she stood there, struck dumb by such an astonishing proposal. With a quick intake of breath, she retorted, "You infuriating man! What has that to do with anything?"

His lordship folded his arms across his chest. "Give me your promise," he commanded.

"Very well, if I must," she said, her voice rising an octave. "I promise I shall attend the theater with you. Now what has happened to Miss Woolcott?"

The marquess leaned negligently against a lamppost

and smiled a bewitching smile. "Not a thing that I know of. I made the whole tale up to get you out of there. You should not be gallivanting around London in a hack, nor preaching sermons at theaters, Miss Pymbroke. Surely one with your superior sense of the proprieties would know it is not ladylike behavior."

Hands on hips, Verity was the picture of righteous indignation. "Oooooh, you tricked me!" Then, recalling herself, she took several deep, calming breaths. "You glib-tongued devil," she said at last, glaring at him.

Lord Carrisworth raised his hands in a deprecating manner. "Please, Miss Pymbroke, do not try to turn me up sweet."

This nonsense and the lively twinkle in his lordship's eyes only incensed her more. "Are you a complete care-for-nobody, my lord? I find it hard to believe someone as astute as Lady Iris could be so taken in."

He reached out and flicked her cheek. "I care about you, of course, Miss Pymbroke. After all," he said, ticking items off on his fingers, "we shall be neighbors, and I have your promise to attend the theater with me, and then there is the fact that I shall be sleeping in your bed. You're so charming when you blush that way, my avenging angel. Naturally, I meant while you are sleeping next door. Are you sure there is not an unmaidenly cast to your mind?" he inquired.

At that moment a fiendish wind blew down the street, depositing a bristling sheet of paper against Verity's skirts. Distracted, she retrieved it, glancing at the content in the most cursory manner. Then, a look of horror crossed her delicate features.

It was one of the print shop caricatures circulating about Town. In it, the marquess was depicted reclining in bed with *two* women. Underneath the lampoon ran a poem:

> Most gentlemen are satisfied, 'tis said,
> To have one mistress warm their bed.
>
> But a certain eligible marquess,
> Just won't be content with less
>
> Than a pair of French turtledoves,
> To have as his light o' loves.
>
> Now, can there be any pleasure on earth,
> Left to be pursued by my Lord Carrisworth?

Verity felt her face flame.

The Marquess of Carrisworth stood at her side viewing the paper over her shoulder. Abruptly, he let out a roar of laughter. Had a man ever been so vilified for a deed he had not done?

Unaware of the marquess's innocence in the situation of the twins, shock and anger lit Verity's face as she turned to him. In a choked voice, she railed, "You laugh at this disgusting lampoon, my lord? It amuses you to know these poor girls' reputations are soiled forever? That all of London knows of your vile behavior?"

A crowd gathered to watch the pretty young girl deliver the aristocrat a scathing set-down.

Beyond caring that she had an audience, Verity pointed an accusing finger at his broad chest. "Do you think it funny you have disgraced your name in this way?"

The marquess chuckled and said, "Really, Miss Pymbroke, you refine too much on the matter. In this age, no gentleman is condemned for pursuing his pleasure."

The assembly snickered and guffawed their agreement. Verity looked at them in disgust. "Perhaps that is a sad truth, sir," she said archly. "In that case, people need to learn that true happiness comes from helping others and from maintaining a pure mind and heart."

Groans and hisses issued from the crowd.

A smile spread across Lord Carrisworth's face. "You see, the multitude are in my corner, dear lady. You would be wise to remember 'Some rise by sin, and some by virtue fall.' "

Digging in her heels in the face of adversity, Miss Pymbroke unwittingly delivered the marquess a verbal facer. "What would your mother think if she saw this sheet of paper?"

Lord Carrisworth's features hardened. "Why damme, I declare she could not say anything about it. Nothing at all."

Verity stared at his unyielding countenance. In the following silence she felt deep mortification grow within herself to mingle with a number of other emotions. Here she was, in the middle of the street, raising her voice like the veriest hoyden. Despite her earlier resolutions not to let the marquess cut up her peace and cause her to behave with less than her usual composure, he had done so again.

"If that is how you truly feel, my lord, I must decline your offer of transport. I would much prefer to find my own way home than to be seen in your company." She turned on her heel and, with her maid trudging along, marched away through the parting crowd.

Seeing the show was over, people began moving on their way, leaving the marquess to stand alone. He shrugged his shoulders thinking he would not have been able to rally quickly enough to protest her departure.

Shouting to his tiger, Lord Carrisworth entered his carriage hell-bent on spending another evening at Mrs. Dantry's becoming thoroughly, disgustingly drunk.

Chapter Three

Having completed her move into Lady Iris's house, Verity was taking care of a few last-minute tasks before turning over the keys to her home to the Marquess of Carrisworth.

With only Empress for company, she was in what had been her father's bedchamber. The cat reposed with half-closed eyes on a massive four-poster, her beautiful silver-gray fur and regal air contrasting with the bed's faded maroon silk hangings.

Verity had ordered a thorough cleaning in anticipation of the marquess's arrival, and the air smelled faintly of beeswax. A mahogany highboy gleamed on one side of the room, and a heavy, dark armoire stood between the two narrow windows that overlooked the mews. His lordship would surely select this masculine bedchamber for his use while leasing the house.

Verity thought back to the contretemps with Lord Carrisworth outside the theater two days ago. Even in the privacy of the room, she blushed when she remembered her too-public display of emotion. Drat the man for oversetting her self-control! But the provocation had been great, she allowed. Another gently bred young girl might have swooned at the contents of that lampoon.

Her heated reproach had been pointless, however. In

the future, she would not waste her time trying to reach the conscience of such a confirmed rake. The scoundrel probably had none.

Dismissing the marquess's character from her mind, Verity looked about her sadly. The room had not been opened since her father's abandonment of his family some thirteen years before when she had been a little girl of six summers. How ironic that another rake would be inhabiting these walls.

She seated herself at the late viscount's Carlton House-style desk and tried to recall a memory of her father in this room, but as always, could not. They had not been close, and most of the sorrow she had endured as a result of his desertion sprang from empathy with her mother's pain, rather than any personal loss. However, as she'd grown, she had wondered what her life would have been like had the viscount stayed and fulfilled his role as father to her.

Giving herself a mental shake, Verity came back to the present from her musings. Anxious to quit the room, she impatiently opened the drawer underneath the leather writing surface in order to remove the viscount's embossed paper, leaving the space free for the marquess's use.

At that moment, Empress hopped from the bed to scurry underneath the desk. The cat began a playful game, jumping in excitement and clawing at the bottom of the drawer.

"What in heaven's name are you doing, Empress?" Verity asked, leaving the drawer open and rising from her seat to see what had caught the cat's attention. Kneeling down, she peered underneath the desk and saw a length of pale blue ribbon hanging suspended from the back of the drawer.

"Oh, Empress," Verity cried with a laugh, "you are a demon when it comes to ribbons."

Empress swiped furiously at the enticing toy in apparent agreement.

"No, I must not allow you to capture it. You might devour it, and then you would be in the suds." Verity grasped the dangling ribbon and quickly pocketed it before Empress could see where it had gone. Giving the cat a scratch behind the ears, she said, "Sorry, your highness, but it is for your own good."

Empress gave the bottom of the drawer a final swipe, turned, and crept from the room, her fluffy tail twitching in frustration.

Verity missed this display of temper, however. Her curiosity had been aroused by the sight of a small drawer, which could be seen from her particular vantage point, worked into the back of the larger drawer. How clever. Only if the larger drawer was open could the secret one be observed.

Ducking under the desk again, she spied a tiny pull, grasped it, and tugged the drawer open. It extended with its opening upside down, and something shiny fell from the hiding place onto the Aubusson carpet at Verity's knees.

She picked it up, closed the drawer, and backed out from under the desk. Sitting on the floor, she examined the object closely.

It was a miniature of a stunningly lovely woman. Her dark curls framed a perfect face marred only by the sadness in her eyes.

Verity felt her heart beat hard. This was not her gentle, brown-haired mother. Nor did it resemble the portrait she had seen of the viscount's first wife, Louisa's fair mother.

Her fingers tightened on the framed likeness of the woman who must have been her father's mistress. The actress he had left his family to run away with, only to be killed in a rough crossing from Ramsgate on the way to Brussels.

"Verity, where are you, dear child?" Lady Hyacinth's voice called from the hallway.

Slipping the miniature into the pocket that contained the ribbon, Verity was still seated on the floor when Lady Hyacinth entered the room clinging to the Marquess of Carrisworth's arm.

Lady Hyacinth immediately assumed the worst. "Oh, Verity! Is something amiss? Never say you have had a spasm at your age. Or was it a knee? Knees can be such pesky things."

"Please do not be concerned, my lady. I simply dropped something under the desk." Embarrassed by her unseemly position, Verity prepared to rise using the desktop as a lever.

But before she could do so, the marquess was at her side. "Here, allow me to assist you, Miss Pymbroke." As he spoke, he reached down, grasped both her hands, and in one swift movement brought her to her feet.

Lady Hyacinth raised a plump hand to her mouth to cover the astonished O of delight that formed. While she was not privy to Lady Iris's scheme for the two, romance was never far from her mind.

Seeing the young people together, her thoughts immediately ran down the gratifying road of a flirtation between the marquess and dear Verity. Lady Hyacinth quickly crossed the room to the side of the bed, ostensibly to be sure the sheets had been aired properly, but really to give the couple a moment alone.

At Lord Carrisworth's nearness Verity's senses spun.

She inhaled the faint lime scent he wore as she noticed that he was the very glass of fashion in his dark blue coat, buff pantaloons, and gleaming Hessian boots. His deep, caressing voice had acted like a magnet to draw her close. A fact that, as a practiced seducer, he was probably well aware of, she abruptly realized.

Verity pulled away from him. "My lord, as I have already informed you, I can look after myself," she said in freezing accents.

A roguish expression came onto the marquess's face. "That did not appear the case with Lord Davies in the Green Room," he said for her ears alone.

Flushing under this truth, Verity sought refuge in a change of subject. "The house is ready for you, Lord Carrisworth. I have had this room aired and cleaned, assuming it would be to your lordship's taste."

The marquess took this gaze from her face with reluctance. She enchanted him with her prim manner. He sensed there was much more beneath her oh-so-proper ways. Perhaps he might spend some time uncovering it. "Was this your father's room?"

"Yes," she replied curtly.

He studied the increased stiffening of her posture when she made her response. "I am sorry. Did your father pass away recently? I have noticed you wear mourning clothes."

Denial flew from her. "It is not for my father that I mourn. He died many years ago after running off with an actress." Contempt turned her normally sweet voice sharp. Then, her eyes widened, and her hand came up over her mouth as if she regretted voicing her father's perfidy aloud.

Ah, thought the marquess. So that explained her mission to reform the actresses of the world. Glancing around him speculatively he said, "Well, I should not make this room my own, then. I believe the pink-and-white apartment at the end of the hall will serve instead."

Verity gasped in dismay. "My lord! That is my room. Surely, with its feminine adornments it would not be fitting."

The marquess shot her a sidelong glance. "Did I not tell you I would be sleeping in your bed?" he asked with maddening self-assurance.

"You cannot be serious. 'Twould not be proper," Verity proclaimed.

"Miss Pymbroke, I believe you are well aware of my feelings regarding what is 'proper.' Besides, you have leased me the house, and it would not be fair of you to dictate which room I may sleep in. Does the thought of me beneath your sheets disturb you so much?"

Verity bit her lip. Mentally, she slammed the door shut on the picture he painted of himself under her pink coverlet.

He was goading her, she knew. Furthermore, it was shabby of him to appeal to her sense of fairness. It seemed the marquess had no scruples when it came to getting his own way. "Please yourself then, my lord. I am certain you will anyway. But this exchange reminds me that there are a few rules for your tenancy I should like to explain before giving you the keys."

Over by the bed, Lady Hyacinth, well and truly disappointed with the couple's unloverlike behavior, walked to Verity's side and said, "Oh, dear child, perhaps you can discuss that over a nice tea tray. I declare I am feeling sharp-set."

Verity frowned at the marquess before turning to smile on her ladyship. "Of course, Lady Hyacinth," she said, stepping forward and placing an arm affectionately around the older woman's shoulders. "Forgive me for not thinking of it myself."

"That's all right, dear. You had other matters on your mind. Or you should have," Lady Hyacinth stated, batting her eyelashes at the marquess like a miss of seventeen.

Some moments later, seated comfortably in the morning room around a heavily laden tea tray, Lady Hyacinth indulged her healthy appetite.

Verity gazed at her fondly before turning to Lord Carrisworth. He was at his leisure, his long, muscular legs stretched out in front of him so she might admire them.

She quickly averted her gaze. Smoothing the folds of her dull brown dress, Verity adopted the attitude of a governess. "Now, my lord, as to the rules I mentioned earlier. There are to be no parties held here during the time you are leasing these premises. In addition, I have rented you the house, but not the garden. Mama toiled over those roses for years before she became ill, and I took over the task since then. I plan to continue maintaining their splendor in her honor, but shall not disturb you as there is a door in the wall of the garden leading to the outside which I shall make use of."

Pausing for breath, Verity noticed the marquess was regarding her with a limpid look. She continued with a hint of unease at the next stipulation. "In addition, I would have none of your . . . paramours here to shock the servants."

A strangled sound escaped from Lord Carrisworth and his shoulders shook.

Lady Hyacinth licked the crumbs of a seed cake from her fingers. "Don't be a goose, Verity. His lordship isn't going to parade any of his doxies here. He'll have set up another house where he can visit them."

The marquess could no longer restrain himself. He wiped his streaming eyes and declared, "Miss Pymbroke, you are a treasure."

Disconcerted, Verity crossed her arms and pointedly looked away.

Lady Hyacinth's gaze lingered appreciatively over his lordship's legs.

Just then, Digby entered the room and intoned, "Mrs. Louisa Barrington."

Verity's long-awaited sister walked into the room. Her pale blonde hair was twisted into an elegant coiffure underneath a dashing plumed bonnet. A cherry-colored velvet spencer topped a cherry-and-ivory striped silk day dress. At two and thirty her face was beginning to take on lines, but these were artfully concealed by cosmetics.

"Louisa!" Verity cried, rushing to embrace her. "Oh, how I have prayed for your return, and here you are at last!"

"Mouse, can it be you?" Louisa queried, using Verity's nursery name. "How you have grown. Careful, lest you crush my gown." Louisa disengaged herself and fastened her cool gray gaze on the marquess, who had risen to his feet at her entrance.

Introductions were hastily performed, and Louisa dropped a curtsy, dismissing Lady Hyacinth, but favoring his lordship with a seductive smile.

When everyone was once again seated around the tea tray, Verity could hardly contain her excitement. "I was ten years old when last we saw each other, Louisa. You and Philip had only been married a few years when he whisked you off to the continent. I was wretched for months! Oh heavens, Louisa, poor, dear Philip.

Even though it has been two years, you must miss him dreadfully."

Louisa took a sip of her tea, a puzzled expression crossing her face for a brief moment. But, it was gone before it could be noticed by anyone but the marquess.

"Yes, the memory of Philip's tragic death still pains me." Louisa produced a wispy lace handkerchief from her velvet reticule and dabbed at her dry eyes.

"Where have you been living, Mrs. Barrington?" the marquess inquired.

Louisa appeared pleased at this show of interest. "Everywhere, my lord, but most recently Spain."

"Spain? We thought you were still in Portugal," Lady Hyacinth said, baffled.

"La, I have become quite the traveler. I enjoy seeing different places, different people. But a desire for all the gaiety of a London Season brought me home."

"Surely you wished to see your sister above anything else," Lord Carrisworth said silkily.

A faint hint of color came into Louisa's cheeks at this reproof. "Naturally, my lord. I dote on my little Mouse."

Lady Hyacinth rose to her feet. "You must be prodigiously weary, Louisa. Traveling is always injurious to one's health. I shall go home and order the room next to Verity's made up for you at once."

The older woman waddled from the room, leaving Louisa mystified. "Has Lady Hyacinth lost her wits? Why should I want to stay with those two old eccentrics?"

Verity shifted uneasily in her chair. "We must stay with the Ladies Iris and Hyacinth, Louisa. You see, for the sake of economy I found it necessary to let the house for the Season. And the ladies are lifelong friends who have been everything that is good to me since Mama's death. I am sorry if you cannot like it, but I had no other choice."

Louisa bridled. She opened her mouth to give her sister a thundering scold, when Lord Carrisworth drawled, "I am forever grateful to Miss Pymbroke for her decision since I shall benefit from it. My own townhouse was damaged by fire, and I found myself at sixes and sevens until she agreed to lease her home to me. I am moving in today."

Louisa's cool gray eyes studied her sister consideringly. "How advantageous. And I would never break squares with Mouse on my first day home."

Verity smiled lovingly at her sister. "Come, I shall give the keys to his lordship, and we can settle in next door. Perhaps we shall stay up half the night catching up with one another's escapades," she ended with a laugh.

The corners of Louisa's mouth turned in at this plan, but Verity was fishing in her reticule for the house keys and therefore missed her sister's expression of chagrin.

Lord Carrisworth accepted the keys from Verity's outstretched hand, taking the opportunity to brush her fingertips with his. Pleased at the heightened color in her cheeks, he said, "Miss Pymbroke, remember you are engaged to go to the playhouse with me this evening."

"The playhouse," Louisa crooned. "How I envy you, Verity."

At the thought of spending an evening in the marquess's company, a suffocating sensation tightened Verity's throat. Then, she stiffened her spine. Her sense of duty forced her to realize one did not give one's word and go back on it no matter how diabolically the promise had been wrung from her.

"Very well, my lord. Tonight it will be. But as you cannot expect me to accompany you alone, I am certain you will want to include Louisa in your invitation, if she is not overtired from her journey."

Louisa's gray eyes glittered. "I am not at all fatigued."

"How fortunate for me," Lord Carrisworth dissembled. For he was not pleased at this turn of events.

Since the conventions never troubled him, he had, indeed, entertained the thought he might have Miss Pymbroke alone. An intriguing sparkle of warmth and affection had come into her velvet brown eyes since her sister's arrival. His lordship found he desired to see Miss Pymbroke gaze upon him so.

In addition, he'd been on the Town too long to be taken in by Mrs. Barrington, seeing through her thin veneer of respectability. He did not for a moment believe the widow had traveled the continent alone on a soldier's pension. More likely, she had recently broken off with a lover and, without another at hand, had been forced to return to England.

None of these reflections showed on his handsome countenance, however. As usual, his manner was flirtatious and carefree while he finalized the arrangements for the evening ahead before showing the ladies to the door.

After they'd gone, Lord Carrisworth gave orders for a light repast and then called himself a fool when he found his thoughts dwelling on what her sister's arrival might mean for Miss Pymbroke's life. In truth, he told himself, the matter was of no interest whatsoever. It was simply that Miss Pymbroke served to alleviate some of his wretched boredom. He found the combination of her Puritan airs and her delectable face and figure amusing.

And to be amused, to find pleasure where he could, were the marquess's sole pursuits in life.

That evening at supper while the conversation centered around Louisa, Lady Iris felt cross. Like the marquess, she had seen Louisa's true nature immediately. The gel had always been selfish and willful, and Lady Iris shrewdly judged the years since Louisa left London had hardened her irrevocably.

Equally obvious was that Verity adored Louisa. Probably because of all that rot she preached about familial bonds, Lady Iris thought in disgust while she watched her own sister shovel food into her mouth at a great rate.

At the end of the meal Lady Hyacinth suddenly groaned and pressed a hand to her stomach. "Bless me! Iris, speak to Cook. The cream sauce must have been rancid, and now I am suffering from a disordered spleen."

Louisa made a moue of distaste.

Verity bestowed a pitying look on Lady Hyacinth. "Dear lady, how unfortunate. Shall I help you upstairs to your bed?"

Lady Iris glared at Lady Hyacinth. "'Tis not the sauce, you ninny. Your appetite rivals that of Heliogabalus, the Roman emperor notorious for his gluttony. Unlace your stays and you'll recover fast enough."

These acid remarks fell on deaf ears, because Lady Hyacinth had risen and was allowing Verity to lead her from the dining room.

Lady Iris finished her wine and turned to Louisa. "I'm sure you want your bed, so I won't keep you."

The subject of the marquess's escort to the playhouse had never come up, the company being immersed in the topic of Louisa's doings, so Lady Iris and Lady Hyacinth remained in ignorance of the plan.

A steely edge came into Lady Iris's voice. "Mind, we're very fond of Verity in this house and would not see her hurt. Keep that thought in your brain box and we'll rub along together well enough."

Louisa lowered her eyes so Lady Iris could not see the wrath reflected in them. "Yes, my lady."

Lady Iris peered at the widow sharply for a moment, then rose. "I have to go to the kitchens. Not to reprimand Cook like Hyacinth wants. Got another reason," she mumbled.

Empress had been lying beside her mistress's chair, but at her departure, trotted over to Louisa to eye her as astutely as Lady Iris had.

Louisa looked down at the animal and said, "Cats are annoying creatures. They belong in the kitchens, catching mice. Go on with you. Shoo!"

Empress flattened her ears and darted from the room.

Louisa sat where she was for a moment, clutching her wineglass until her fingers whitened.

Things were not as she had expected on her return. Trust Verity's silly Mama not to have remarried in order to provide for her family, Louisa thought uncharitably. Her own Mama had been too cunning to have ever allowed herself to reach such a pass. If only she'd lived, Louisa wished, not for the first time. The very idea of having to stay in this house with two horrible, ancient ladies. Pah!

At least the handsome Marquess of Carrisworth was right next door. Now there was a man, Louisa reflected. She would wager he knew exactly how to please a woman in bed. A smile curved her lips while she imagined the marquess's hands roaming her naked body, and hers caressing his.

She had learned a great deal about men's bodies and how to use their desires to her advantage since her husband died—and some before he had left this earth. But she was growing older and must make another marriage before it was too late. The trouble was, all the eligible gentlemen on the continent seemed aware of her fondness for variety in her bed partners. She had needed to come home to England where her reputation was intact to secure a husband.

And what better testimony to her own virtue than her naive little sister. Lud, how Verity had changed over the years. She had been a happy, carefree child, but had grown into a sanctimonious prude. How she had gone on with her moralizing before supper! It was all to the good, however. It wouldn't do to have her pretty, much younger sister outshine her.

The sounds of Lady Iris shouting curses, and another female, whom Louisa assumed was the Cook, caterwauling finally sent her upstairs to prepare for her evening at the playhouse.

Verity dismissed Lady Hyacinth's abigail and ran the warming pan herself over the lady's mattress. Lady Hyacinth selected one of the many bottles of medicines from the table next to the bed, poured herself a large dose, then grimaced when she swallowed the contents.

Tucking the older woman in bed and making sure she was comfortable, Verity made as if to leave the room in order to ready herself for the evening, but Lady Hyacinth wanted to talk.

"Thank you, dear child, you are an excellent creature.

It will be splendid having someone in the house who understands my sensibilities. Iris never has."

Verity adjusted the bed hangings. "My lady, I shall not hear a word against your sister tonight. If it were not for her idea for me to lease my house, I do not know what I should have done."

Lady Hyacinth sighed dreamily and patted her red hair. "Yes, isn't the marquess spectacular? Such legs."

Verity compressed her lips into a thin line.

Unknowingly echoing Louisa's earlier thoughts, her ladyship continued, "He impresses me as the sort who would strip to advantage. Puts me in mind of the Earl of Marsh back in 1777. Or was it '78? No matter. Not that I ever saw the earl without his shirt, but he knew to a nicety how to diddle with a gel's bubbies. Most pleasing."

Verity made her excuses as fast as possible after Lady Hyacinth's improbable reminiscences and fled to her bedchamber where she bathed her hot cheeks with cool water.

The sisters had given her a lovely room, done in olive green with white and peach accents. Verity seated herself at a satinwood dressing table.

The same maid who'd accompanied Verity to the theater was flipping through the gowns in a large armoire. She was the only servant Verity had taken from the house next door. "What will you be wearin' to the playhouse this evenin', miss? There's nothin' here that's right for such a grand evenin'. You'll want to look your best for his lordship. Ever so handsome, he is."

"Fustian!" Verity exclaimed, out of reason cross. Must everyone expound on the marquess's attractive person? No doubt, he would share their views if he but heard them.

"Betty, I am not going to the playhouse to impress his

lordship, thus it matters not what I wear. I . . . I am going on the hope I might perceive some clue as how best to reach the actresses spiritually. So far, I have not been successful in convincing any of them of their folly."

Betty looked doubtful. "Yes, miss."

"The lavender with the black trim will serve," Verity informed her. The gown she selected was another severe style of half-mourning, with long sleeves and a high neck.

The maid helped her mistress undress. Verity stood clad only in a scant, very lacy shift. For one whose clothes were modest in the extreme, the garment was vastly out of character.

But Verity's one vanity was that she adored feminine undergarments. After washing in rose-scented water, she pulled on fine silk stockings and lashed them tightly to her legs with a pair of red silk garters.

Betty's suggestion that Verity soften her hairstyle for the evening was swiftly refused. After scraping a final pin through her hair, to be certain not a single tendril escaped its knot, Verity hurried out of the room, leaving Betty to heave an exasperated sigh.

Out on the landing, Verity stopped short, and her mouth dropped open in surprise at the sight of her sister who was preparing to descend the staircase. Louisa was clad in an ice blue satin gown, its bodice cut low, revealing an indecent amount of flesh. About her neck flashed an expensive diamond necklace.

"What is it, Mouse?" Louisa inquired, her gray eyes reflecting a cynical amusement at her sister's appraisal.

Verity closed her gaping mouth and stepped closer to her sister. As she did, she saw Louisa had darkened her pale eyelashes with lamp black. Cosmetics! Verity's lips pursed in disapproval.

The sounds of Bingwood admitting a caller reached their ears. Wishing to make her entrance in front of the marquess alone, Louisa said, "Run on down, Verity, I have forgotten my shawl."

"Thank goodness you intend on wearing something to cover yourself," Verity murmured, but Louisa had turned on her heel and headed in the direction of her room, missing the comment.

As Verity walked down the stairs, her mind reeled with questions. Where had Louisa obtained such lavish finery? That necklace must be worth a fortune.

And she must speak with her sister about her appearance. While there was no doubt in Verity's mind Louisa was the beauty of the family, she needed to adopt a more chaste mode of dress. Verity knew it was her Christian duty to explain to her sister that, while she was certain it was not Louisa's intention, she was flaunting her looks.

Her expression troubled, Verity reached the bottom of the stairs. She'd been so wrapped up in her thoughts, she had failed to notice the Marquess of Carrisworth standing in the hall watching her, a shimmer of amusement visible in his eyes.

"Good evening, Miss Pymbroke. What an interesting choice of gown for the theater."

Any response Verity might have made died unspoken on her lips. Her eyes widened in astonishment because Lord Carrisworth stood before her in all the glory of his evening clothes.

A charcoal-gray coat fit his athletic body to perfection. His cravat was a sculptured miracle of snow-white cloth. A large emerald, which Verity thought paled in comparison with his lordship's green eyes, nestled in its folds. A figured white waistcoat and black silk breeches completed the picture of aristocratic elegance.

Lady Hyacinth's and Betty's words about the marquess being handsome floated across her brain.

Verity's eyes met Lord Carrisworth's and she held his gaze, swallowing hard.

Very well, then. This was to be a challenge to the high moral standards she embraced. Her resolve strengthened. Tonight, at the playhouse, she would show Lord Carrisworth how little his devastating good looks affected her. She raised her chin.

His lordship's gaze abruptly swung to the staircase. He made his bow to Louisa, smiling pleasantly. "You do not look at all tired from your journey, Mrs. Barrington."

Louisa determined to ignore the weakness of this compliment and set herself to flirting with Lord Carrisworth during the journey to the theater, a circumstance the marquess seemed to accept with cool equanimity.

Verity endured the drive, her arms folded across her chest, and stared out into the dark night. It would be her responsibility to apprise her sister of his lordship's nature. Of course, having only just arrived in Town, Louisa could not be expected to know of the marquess's wicked ways.

Lord Carrisworth had determined Louisa to be that most dangerous female, a widow on the prowl for a husband. He was relieved when, arriving at the Theatre Royal, he noticed his friend, Sir Ramsey. "Randy! Care to join my party? Let me make you known to these two charming ladies."

Sir Ramsey made an elegant bow while his puzzled gaze ran over Verity's gown and coiffure. His hazel eyes brightened, however, when they rested on Mrs.

Barrington. He offered her his arm immediately and engaged her in a conversation about her travels.

As the marquess had hoped, Louisa recovered at once from his own lack of interest under the flattering attentions of Sir Ramsey. The two trailed behind, having to stop when Louisa discovered she had dropped her fan.

Thus, Verity and Lord Carrisworth entered his box alone. The marquess had wisely timed their arrival after the often bawdy one-act play that usually preceded a Shakespearean tragedy.

But he had not spared a thought for Society's reaction to seeing London's premier rake accompanied by such a Puritan-looking female. Quizzing glasses were raised. Opera glasses were trained on the pair. Some young bucks went so far as to stand on their chairs, hoping for a better view.

Surely a man who had kept a string of dashing high-flyers and was currently the protector of two mistresses who were twins, a four-bottle man, a man unerringly blessed with luck at Fortune's sportive wheel and whose horses could trot against anything alive, would have no real interest in a woman like the one at his side.

As fans fluttered and whispering reached a peak, the general consensus was the Marquess of Carrisworth was roasting them.

Standing next to him, Verity felt miserable for the marquess. She was certain all the attention being given them was due to those dreadful lampoons circulating. Even though his lordship had brought the censure on himself, she found her tender heart touched with sympathy at his humiliation.

She turned to him, her eyes filled with pity. "My lord, you must rise above such condemnation. You have learned your lesson, I think, and will behave more admirably in the future. I suggest, as a beginning, you send those two unfortunate French girls to a convent."

Chapter Four

Laughter formed in the back of Lord Carrisworth's throat at Miss Pymbroke's assertions, but he suppressed it while gazing down at her earnest face. A quiet voice inside him said if she knew the truth, that it was she who was at the center of Society's whispers, then hurt would be reflected in her brown eyes which, for the first time, were looking upon him with tenderness.

The marquess decided he quite liked being the recipient of Miss Pymbroke's compassion, and so he reached out a gloved hand and gave her cheek a careless pat. "Thank you. But I do not care one jot what people are saying."

Behind them, Louisa and Sir Ramsey entered the box. Lord Carrisworth saw everyone seated comfortably before sitting down himself. Louisa and Sir Ramsey glanced around the theater at the interested faces of the various notables watching their box and began a whispered conversation.

The marquess was happy to see the widow occupied. It left him free to converse with Miss Pymbroke. "I hope you will enjoy the play. It is *Romeo and Juliet*."

Diverted, Verity turned her gaze to the stage. "I must admit, 'tis one of my favorites."

"Ah, you are a romantic, then. Do not deny it," he said

swiftly. "It may interest you to know it was here in 1779 that Prinny first saw Mary Robinson. And, in 1791, his brother, the Duke of Clarence, met Mrs. Jordan." He smiled seductively, leaned close to her, and murmured, "Many great love affairs have begun in this theater. Perhaps another will commence tonight."

Verity folded her gloved hands in her lap. "You are speaking of illicit relationships, my lord, ones not sanctioned by the church. I have no desire to converse about such immoral conduct."

Deliberately misunderstanding her, Lord Carrisworth said smoothly, "You have no desires? When I look into the velvet depths of your eyes, Miss Pymbroke, I find that hard to believe."

Those same eyes smoldered dangerously when Verity said, "Sir, you are impertinent. Our connection exists only because you are leasing my townhouse. I would thank you to remember I am here this evening because of a promise you extracted from me, and ask you to cease these practiced compliments."

The marquess replied to this request with mocking gallantry. "I shall obey you in this, as in everything, my landlady."

As the play began, he sat back to enjoy Miss Pymbroke's reaction.

In the beginning, her face was set, and he imagined her mind working on the problem of reforming the actresses.

But slowly, as the story progressed, he could tell she had been drawn into the plight of the characters. She leaned forward in her chair in rapt attention, seemingly oblivious to her surroundings. During the tragic ending, when Juliet thrust the knife into herself, tears trembled on Miss Pymbroke's long eyelashes before falling to travel down her ivory cheeks. She reached into her reticule and produced a dainty handkerchief.

Fascinated by her refreshingly genuine response, the marquess never took his gaze from her.

They did not stay for the afterpiece, Lord Carrisworth judging it best to leave while Miss Pymbroke was still plainly moved by the performance. As they made their way toward the waiting coach, she appeared remote and distracted.

The marquess handed Miss Pymbroke into the vehicle, watching Sir Ramsey taking a prolonged leave from Mrs. Barrington. The baronet could be seen raising the widow's hand to his lips and kissing it for what seemed an overlong time.

Carrisworth noted the look of disapproval on Miss Pymbroke's lovely face. Deciding the pair had gone on long enough, he called to his friend. "Randy, will I see you at White's later on?"

Sir Ramsey broke away from Louisa with obvious reluctance. "I am not moving from this spot until Mrs. Barrington says she will be at the Foxworths' breakfast tomorrow."

Louisa gave a practiced trill of laughter. "La, sir, I have not been invited anywhere yet."

"What has that to say to anything, my dear Mrs. Barrington? I daresay Lady Iris has received a card, and as her guest you must be included. Say you will go, else I shall stand in Brydges Street all night," Sir Ramsey warned.

Louisa cast him a coy look. "Very well, I shall attend, but only if you give me your escort. Lady Iris may have sent her regrets, and I should not like you to wait for me in vain. You might find another lady upon whom to bestow your attentions."

"Never!" Sir Ramsey assured her. "I shall consider it an honor to escort you and shall call for you at three." With a final bow he turned and walked toward his own carriage, whistling a jaunty tune as he went.

Inside Lord Carrisworth's comfortable coach, Verity drew in her breath sharply. Louisa's behavior was really too bad. Before long, if her sister was not careful, she would be labeled fast.

Louisa settled in the seat next to Verity, and the coach set out over the cobblestone streets. Presently, Verity was brought out of her musings by the marquess. "Did you enjoy the play, Miss Pymbroke?" he asked quietly.

Verity's innate honesty forced her to be candid. "Yes, my lord. I confess it was like nothing I have ever experienced. I felt transported to another time and place. It was delightful."

"And would you not agree, the actresses savor their performances onstage? That they consider what they do an art?"

Verity looked up to see if he was taunting her. But his face merely reflected a polite interest. "They seem proud of their profession," she admitted. "No wonder they would not listen to my urgings for them to find another means of making their living."

Louisa broke her silence to ask incredulously, "You've been moralizing to a group of actresses? How could you be so silly, Verity?"

Verity's hands twisted the strings of her reticule. "Father left us for an actress . . ." she whispered.

"Lud, that wasn't Mary Jennings's fault. Father had his own weaknesses and made his own decisions," Louisa stated with the air of one to whom the matter had long since been resolved.

"Mary Jennings, was that her name?" Verity asked,

the likeness painted on the miniature springing into her mind.

"She was the one named at the time by the tattle-baskets," Louisa replied with a yawn.

Lord Carrisworth said gently, "Miss Pymbroke, most of the actresses have no home to return to, no family capable of providing for them. And, as you saw tonight, even if they did, they would probably choose to remain where they are. Think on it and see if you can still find it in your heart to condemn them."

Verity experienced a gamut of perplexing emotions. Under the marquess's steady scrutiny, she could barely think. This serious side to him caused her heart to beat hard.

For some reason, when he spoke thoughtfully, she found his appeal much stronger. When he was clearly flirting, she found it much easier to resist his charms. But this glimpse of a sincere, unaffected demeanor drew her to him, frightening her.

She was grateful when the coach stopped in front of Lady Iris's and could have screamed in frustration when Louisa asked his lordship to share their tea tray and the invitation was accepted.

Entering the drawing room, the party found Lady Iris sitting on the dark blue settee, attended by the sisters' maid, Beecham.

Her ladyship took one look at Verity's gown and stomped her cane on the floor so hard that Empress, curled in her mistress's lap, awoke with a start. The cat jumped from Lady Iris's lap to the floor, her slanted blue eyes glaring at the company in reproach for this disturbance.

"By Jupiter, Verity, Beecham tells me you went to the theater tonight. How could you have gone out dressed like the lowest parson's daughter? If you've taken it into your head to go about in Society—and it's past time you did—you must be properly gowned first."

Verity bristled. "I would like to go out more. But, must appearances count for so much? I do not believe in improving overmuch on what the Good Lord has given me."

"He didn't give you that gown," Lady Iris howled. "You had it off some unfashionable dressmaker."

"Good evening, Lady Iris. Mrs. Barrington promised me a tea tray," said Lord Carrisworth, trying to divert the elderly woman's attention while everyone sat down.

"Bring the damn tea tray, Beecham," Lady Iris commanded, her gaze moving from one person to the other as if trying to fix blame for the social solecism committed by her young friend.

As the hour was late, Louisa forgot for a moment that Verity's appearance suited her purposes. She was goaded into saying, "You should have seen the way people laughed and stared at Mouse at the theater. I declare they all thought it was a rare joke."

Verity's mouth dropped open in astonishment at the revelation it was she, and not the marquess, who had garnered the unsavory attention.

Seeing Miss Pymbroke's crestfallen expression, Lord Carrisworth experienced a strong desire to slap Mrs. Barrington's face. Instead, he decided to raise Miss Pymbroke's ire. That would at least remove that wounded look in her brown eyes he was finding he could not bear.

He raised his quizzing glass, studying the dress in question. Then he quickly dropped it, as if in disgust. "It is a perfectly horrid gown, Miss Pymbroke. Surely your year of mourning is over. You are one to follow rules.

What do the rules state regarding when a lady may put off her blacks?"

The marquess was content with the swift shadow of anger that swept across her face. She had no chance to respond to him, though, because Lady Iris had found a person she could hold responsible for her young friend's attire.

"Louisa, I'd have thought you, as Verity's *loving* sister, would have instructed her as to how to dress, mayhaps lent her a gown."

Seeing the look of offended hauteur crossing Louisa's features, Lady Iris pressed her point. "Yes, Louisa, now that I think on it, you will want to share your gowns with Verity. Beecham tells me you had four trunks' worth of 'em for her to unpack, so you won't care a rush about giving half of them to Verity. She can't afford new ones and won't allow me to help her. Of course, Beecham will have to make them over to fit her, Verity being better endowed than you, but then at your age everything begins to droop."

From her position on the floor, Empress miaowed in evident agreement.

Louisa rose, her color heightened. Unable to trust herself not to tell Lady Iris exactly what she could do with her ideas she said stiffly, "I shall select some gowns for my sister in the morning."

Verity stood and embraced Louisa. "Thank you. You are the best of sisters."

Hearing this statement, Lord Carrisworth and Lady Iris exchanged apprehensive looks.

Louisa broke away from Verity and curtsyed to his lordship. "Good night, my lord." In her haste to quit the room she nearly collided with a footman carrying the tea tray.

Lady Iris turned her attention to the marquess. "Carrisworth, in future I expect you to request my permission to escort Verity about. I know she's not my ward, but she's living under my roof and needs guidance."

"Very well, my lady," the marquess replied with easy grace. He accepted a cup from Verity and asked, "Do you go to the Foxworths' tomorrow? Mrs. Barrington is being escorted by Sir Ramsey, and I should be happy to drive you as well as Lady Hyacinth and Miss Pymbroke."

In the act of preparing a cup for Lady Iris, Verity ground her teeth in exasperation. "I beg your pardon, my lady, but are my wishes not to be taken into account?"

"No," Lady Iris said baldly. Then her gruff voice softened. "It's been over a year since your Mama was consigned to her tomb. You needn't be covering yourself in mourning clothes or staying home for the rest of your life. You should be around people your own age, having fun. That's what's wrong with your generation. You're mealy-mouthed and don't know how to have a good time."

With a perfectly bland expression, Lord Carrisworth said, "How right you are, Lady Iris. Perhaps together, Miss Pymbroke and I might somehow contrive."

Verity frowned at the marquess, but before she could say anything, a scream pierced the air. Another quickly followed, catapulting the company up the stairs to find their source.

The marquess was first in the upstairs hallway. He followed the sounds of the continued screeching and flung open the door from which they emanated. It was Louisa's bedchamber, and she stood by the fireplace, white-faced with terror. In her hand, she held a heavy poker.

Verity and Beecham arrived with a breathless Lady

Iris on their heels. The trio rushed into the room full of questions. Louisa stood mute, using the poker to point toward the four-poster bed.

Lord Carrisworth crossed the room and let out a derisive laugh. "Is this what all the wailing is about, madam?"

The bedclothes had been turned back for the night, and on one of the pillows lay a dead mouse.

A chuckle escaped from Beecham before she moved forward to remove the offensive sight. Lady Iris barked out a laugh, muttering about how they weren't so missish in her day, and Verity was left to comfort her sister.

But anger had replaced Louisa's fear. She glanced across the room and saw Empress framed in the doorway, a triumphant expression on her feline face. "That horrible cat did this deliberately to spite me. After dinner I told it to go away and catch mice, and look what it did! It is a nasty creature and should be kept below-stairs if not thrown out into the streets."

"What . . . did . . . you . . . say?" Lady Iris demanded, glaring at the widow.

"Oh," Louisa cried, bursting into false tears in hopes his lordship would console her.

Unmoved, the marquess promptly said, "I cannot abide a watering pot. I shall see myself out." He bowed to Lady Iris, informing her he would call to escort them to the breakfast tomorrow at three.

Raising Verity's gloved hand to his lips, he pressed a brief kiss upon it. He stared into her flushed face for just a moment. Then he was gone.

Lady Iris picked Empress up and slung her pet over her shoulder where the cat cast Louisa a feline grin while riding out of the room on her comfortable perch. Lady

Iris's gruff voice could barely be heard in the hall. "How about a dish of cream to wet your whiskers, Empress?"

After Beecham had changed the pillowcase, Louisa was left alone with Verity.

"Dear sister, let me help you into your night rail. You have suffered a shock and would be better for some rest. I am persuaded I should have asked Beecham to bring you some hot milk before I dismissed her," Verity said, fussing with the tapes to Louisa's gown.

Louisa's temper snapped. She flung Verity's hands away. "Go away and leave me in peace, Miss Do-good. I cannot bear your moralizing now, and I can tell you are ready to launch into a sermon."

Verity had been ready to do just that, thinking of Louisa's use of cosmetics, the low cut of her gown, and her bold manner with Sir Ramsey. But she shrank from the look in her sister's eyes, contenting herself by saying, "Your nerves are overset. We shall say our prayers together and then—"

"Out!" Louisa shrieked.

Verity hurried out, cringing when her sister slammed the door after her. She leaned against the wall, breathing deeply.

One thought crystallized in her brain. It was her duty to guide her sister toward more virtuous ways. She might have to give up as lost her mission with the actresses. But here was someone closer to her who was important.

A soft glow came into Verity's dark brown eyes. Louisa needed her help.

And if Verity had to accept the Marquess of Carrisworth's escort in order to help her sister, she simply would have to make the sacrifice.

* * *

The next morning, Lady Iris stood by the pantry in the kitchen. She held a very large reticule, more like a poacher's sack, into which she was stuffing the small bottles of liquid she'd spent the previous evening preparing.

When finished with her task, Lady Iris pulled the hood of a drab cloak down low over her veiled head, which— for once—was not adorned with her customary white wig.

She slipped out the servants' entrance in the rear of the house and into the crisp morning air.

Next door, the Marquess of Carrisworth, having returned from an unaccustomed but refreshing morning ride, had just finished changing his coat. He was standing at an upstairs window contemplating how he would amuse himself this day, when he glanced down and spied the furtive figure of Lady Iris.

Now what is she up to? he thought. He turned away from the pink curtains and picked up a pair of York tan gloves.

Mr. Wetherall, who was neatly stacking foot-wide, newly laundered cravats into an armoire, said, "My lord, I must say this bedchamber is most unsuitable."

"Nonsense, man," his lordship replied, rapidly pulling on the gloves. "My hat and stick, if you please."

Wetherall handed the requested items over to his master, his left eye twitching with disapproval. "But this is a lady's room, my lord. It is not appropriate for one of your consequence to sleep on a bed topped with a pink coverlet."

The marquess's lips twisted in a grin. "On the contrary, I often frequent beds sporting pink coverlets, as you well know."

When his master reached the door, Mr. Wetherall

called out, "My lord! Do you not wish me to call a groom or footman to accompany you?"

But Lord Carrisworth was already out of earshot, leaving his long-suffering valet to cluck his tongue in disapproval. Sighing heavily, Mr. Wetherall consoled himself with the thought that his lordship had not come home in his cups last night. It had been the first such occurrence in quite some time. Mayhap the puppy would finally be done with what Mr. Wetherall charitably termed his lordship's youthful frolics and settle down.

Meanwhile, the marquess followed Lady Iris at a careful distance through the Mayfair streets until he saw her step into an apothecary and herb shop. He waited outside, pretending an interest in the colorful bottles displayed in the window.

A few minutes later, when Lady Iris stomped out of the shop, still clutching her heavy bag, the marquess casually strolled inside and faced the proprietor.

This shrewd merchant, recognizing a member of the Nobility, bowed low. "How my I serve yer honor?"

"You may tell me what business you conducted with the veiled lady just here."

The fat shop owner grimaced and said, "That one! Thinks I don't know who she is, but ye can't fool ole Jack Millweed. Trying to clear her sister's account by sellin' me some home-brewed potion she called 'Love's Helping Hand.' Imagine that, milord! Why, I'd be in a mort o' trouble selling them bottles without the proper tax stamp, no less not knowin' what's in the stuff."

Mr. Millweed then winked lewdly. "She did say the elixir would cause the most unloverlike person to become energetic, but . . ."

The marquess was making a heroic attempt at concealing his amusement. Love's Helping Hand? Lady Iris was concocting some sort of aphrodisiac? By God, the woman was a Trojan.

Then his lordship's thoughts grew solemn. Lady Iris must truly be in need of money to go to such lengths.

He produced a roll of coins and instructed the shopkeeper. "You are to send a discreet note round to the lady's house. You are to apologize and say you will buy whatever she can supply you with. Send me word when she delivers the potions. I expect you to give the lady half this amount, you may keep the rest."

The marquess scribbled a generous figure on the back of one of his cards, then passed it and several of the coins to the stunned Mr. Millweed. "Here is something for your trouble today."

Confident his orders would be obeyed without question, he turned and left the shop.

At precisely three of the clock, Verity stood in the drawing room awaiting the sisters. After a morning of diligent cutting and sewing, Beecham had triumphantly produced one of Louisa's gowns, worked over to fit Verity.

The dress was of peach blossom-colored muslin. Matching ribbon had been used for banding around the high waist and the deep, square-cut neck. The skirt was rather full, and the sleeves were long and tight-fitting.

Beecham, who'd been itching to get her hands on Verity's hair, with Betty's help had finally succeeded in cajoling the girl into allowing a softer style, the front being snipped and curled round her face. Peach-colored ribbon had been worked through the curls that fell from a topknot. The maids had fussed over their charge until both beamed with the becoming results of their efforts.

Uncomfortable with her more modish appearance,

Verity moved to stand in front of a large gilt-trimmed pier glass. She had found a lace fichu and was fidgeting with it, feeling her gown was cut too low.

Tying the material ineffectually around her neck, she was caught off guard when she saw the tall figure of Lord Carrisworth reflected in the mirror. She whirled round, her hands holding the fichu against her breasts in a protective manner, and stared with wide brown eyes at his elegant appearance in a dark green coat.

He raised his quizzing glass and studied her boldly. "No, no, Miss Pymbroke, that ugly piece of lace quite spoils the lines of your fetching gown."

Before she knew what he intended, he crossed the room and removed the offending material. Her hands fell to her sides, and he stared down in evident satisfaction at her creamy neck and the just-visible rise of her bosom.

The heavy lids of his green eyes closed halfway and he murmured, "Better. Much better."

His long, white fingers had brushed Verity's sensitive skin when he removed the fichu. At his touch, she felt her pulse beat erratically in her throat. His deep voice and his closeness completely unnerved her. She felt the invisible web of attraction building between them and could not find her voice.

Lord Carrisworth's gaze remained fixed on the enticing expanse of flesh before him. He experienced a moment of sheer lust.

He lowered his dark head toward her soft shoulder.

Verity closed her eyes.

Bingwood's strident voice rang out in the quiet room. "Sir Ramsey Bertrand."

Verity's eyes flew open, and a tide of red rose to her face. She saw the marquess had moved and was standing at his ease, pouring out a measure of claret.

He handed the glass to her, and while she made it a rule never to drink anything stronger than lemonade, Verity found herself sipping the wine gratefully.

"Sir Ramsey," she said somewhat shakily when she was able, and curtsyed. Her initial impression of the baronet had not been favorable, and she had marked him down as one of the marquess's rakish friends.

The Ladies Iris and Hyacinth walked into the room at that moment followed by Louisa, sophisticated in pale green. Verity used the ensuing exchange of introductions and greetings to regain her composure.

Her flush had receded, leaving two red spots on her white cheeks. What had she done? She had been about to yield to Lord Carrisworth's advances!

She was assailed by a wave of humiliation and regret. To become enamored of him was unthinkable. Had not her mother shown her the pain a rake could inflict upon those who loved him? And what about those two French girls he had under his protection?

Stealing a glance at his lordship's calm demeanor, Verity thought he was, no doubt, laughing inwardly at her behavior. Shifting her gaze to Louisa, who was flirting with Sir Ramsey to a nicety with her fan, Verity viewed the need to correct her sister as crucial. No more of her time could be wasted on considering her feelings for the marquess.

The issue of who was to ride with whom to the Foxworths' villa in Kensington arose. Sir Ramsey had brought an open carriage.

Lady Hyacinth declared, "Never shall I be brought to ride in such a vehicle. Why, the wind rushing through one's ears to one's very brain—it is unthinkable. Not to mention the numerous diseases floating in the air one might be subjected to when traveling through Town."

Verity said quickly, "I shall go with Louisa and Sir Ramsey." She ignored Louisa's disgruntled look and, with her chin raised, swept past Lord Carrisworth, judging he was past all bearing when she heard him chuckle.

The Foxworths took the first syllable of their title name quite seriously and had made the fox their family emblem. Therefore, foxes peered out at visitors from the cloth covering the settee and matching chairs, foxes looked down from the gilt-ornamented frieze, and their eyes watched from the painted ceiling.

Lady Foxworth was a country girl at heart, and as her one concern in entertaining was her guests' comfort, she was a popular hostess.

Cloth-covered tables, laden with meats, fruits, breads, and pastries, had been set out in the garden beyond the saloon. The day was chilly and a bit breezy. The ladies' gauzy draperies fluttered, and the liveried servants had to keep adjusting the cloths on the table which were wont to fly up and cover the food.

Inside, a large fire blazed cheerfully in the huge stone fireplace, jealously guarded by the iron foxes on the andirons. People were standing in groups chatting.

Entering the room, Verity was startled when she discovered Mr. Cecil Sedgewick talking to a rather plain girl with a frightfully long, thin nose. It was unlike the Mr. Sedgewick whom Verity knew to attend Society functions. But, what was most disturbing was the light-hearted air that characterized the gentleman's normally staid features.

Perceiving her scrutiny, Mr. Sedgewick met her gaze with no less surprise at her presence than Verity had been with his. He bowed and she moved to his side.

"Miss Pymbroke, how delightful to see you," he babbled somewhat guiltily.

Mr. Cecil Sedgewick was fully aware of Verity's hopes in his direction regarding marriage. While her admiration fueled his pride, and he approved of her rules and principles and appreciated her beauty, he had no intention of making such an unprofitable alliance.

The aspiring cleric was in need of a living, and should he be fortunate enough to attract a wealthy peer's daughter, he would jump at the chance of securing his future, if not by marriage, then by ingratiating himself with the family. Hence his flattering interest in the antidote standing next to him. "Lady Althea, may I present Miss Verity Pymbroke? Miss Pymbroke, Lady Althea is Lord and Lady Foxworth's daughter."

Verity curtsyed.

After merely giving a nod in return, Lady Althea studied Verity down the great length of her nose. She listlessly plied her fan. "Pymbroke? Oh, yes, the late Viscount Eldon, of course. How unfortunate." The fan flicked in dismissal.

Verity's bosom swelled with indignation at this slur, however justified, at her father's name. She turned to Mr. Sedgewick, but she would get no help from that quarter as he had edged away slightly and was studying a tapestry of foxes with unparalleled interest.

At that moment, the Marquess of Carrisworth appeared at her side. He bowed to Lady Althea, who simpered and snapped open her fan, flirting in what she thought a killing way over its top.

"Would you excuse us, Lady Althea," Lord Carrisworth said in such a regretful tone that Lady Althea must have been certain he could hardly bear to leave her side. "I promised Lady Iris I would look after Miss Pymbroke, and I am persuaded she would appreciate a little something to eat."

Before Verity could denounce this plan, Mr. Sedgewick turned round, all affronted dignity, saying, "I shall bring Miss Pymbroke a plate of her favorites."

"No, you will not," Lord Carrisworth said mildly, and taking Verity's arm, led her away.

They reached the table outside before Verity said, "High-handed! And I shall have you know I am not hungry."

Lord Carrisworth filled a plate and passed it to her. For himself, he took only some champagne. He found a little bench, and they sat down.

"You must eat something to fortify yourself for the lecture you are about to read me." His lordship sighed and took a sip of the bubbling liquid. "I fear I am not always a gentleman."

"Not always a gentleman?" she echoed hotly. "I have yet to see you behave as you should. You inveigled your way into leasing my house when you knew I did not want you as a tenant. Then you tricked me into going with you to the theater, not to mention the unwanted assault you almost made on my person—when, had not Bingwood interrupted, you w-would . . ." Her voice died away, and she turned her head from him in obvious embarrassment.

The marquess gazed at her profile. What was it about this beautiful, but serious, girl that made him want to keep her by his side? She amused him, that was it, he reminded himself firmly and took another sip of champagne.

"Let us forget all that for a moment, Miss Pymbroke. I shall play the part of a gentleman, for once, and refrain from suggesting that, earlier today in the drawing room at Lady Iris's, you did not do anything to deter me, such as slap my face."

Her head swung round, the breeze ruffling her curls, and she glared at him.

"That is better. It is so troublesome for me to talk seriously with you when your face is averted. Now, I noticed you are nursing a *tendre* for Mr. Sedgewick—Begad, Miss Pymbroke, I am certain Lady Hyacinth would have something to say about the injuries you will sustain if your blood continues rushing to your face in that manner. In any event, to show you my appreciation for all your kindness to me, I shall help you catch Mr. Sedgewick."

He ended this speech with a confident smile.

She gripped her plate, her knuckles whitening. "Catch Mr. Sedgewick? How dare you speak to me thus?"

"Though I believe you, as a viscount's daughter, might look higher than a mere mister," he mused aloud, ignoring her question.

Miss Pymbroke's back stiffened. "There can be no gentleman with a *higher tone of mind* than Mr. Sedgewick."

"No? There I believe you are out. If I do not mistake the matter, your Mr. Sedgewick is toadying quite dreadfully to Lady Althea and her mother in the hopes of obtaining a living. They have a snug little parish in Derbyshire."

He saw a flicker of doubt cross her face.

She pursed her lips, then spoke in a low voice, "If I become affianced to Mr. Sedgewick, I should consider myself blessed. He is kind and trustworthy. One cannot expect more from marriage."

The marquess raised a dark eyebrow. "It would not be a love-match? You surprise me. I should have thought a romantic such as yourself to be head and ears, heart and soul in love to contemplate marriage."

"As I told you at the theater, I am not a romantic!"

He lifted a languid hand and wound one of her golden-brown curls around his finger. By God, this new hairstyle was enchanting. His gaze dropped to her rose-pink lips, and he said, "I do not believe you."

She drew in her breath sharply.

He released the strand of hair. "No matter. I have made up my mind to assist you, and I am well qualified to do so. After all, I know what a man finds attractive in a woman. And, with my help, you could be far more appealing to Mr. Sedgewick than even that snug church."

"Thank you," she said dryly and frowned at him.

"There you are! How can you expect to lead any gentleman to the altar when you ruin your beautiful face by scowling like that?" he pointed out reasonably.

The heavy lashes that shadowed her cheeks flew up. "I am not the beauty of the family. Louisa is."

Faith! Was it possible the chit did not know her looks were superior? Well, she would soon learn if she continued to go about in Society. All the young bucks would be after the angelic Miss Pymbroke.

The marquess suddenly glowered into his empty champagne glass. "Mrs. Barrington looks well enough in her way," he said at last.

But he saw Miss Pymbroke's attention had been caught by the sight of her sister standing at the refreshment table in the company of none other than Lord Davies. The widow's tinkling laugh floated across the garden.

Lord Carrisworth sensed, rather than saw, Miss Pymbroke was ready to jump up and rescue her sister from the gentleman who had rudely accosted her in the Green Room at the Theatre Royal. He twisted round in his seat to face her, reached a long arm out, and grasped the arm of the bench, effectively trapping her between it and his body.

"No, Miss Pymbroke, you must not. To accuse Lord Davies in public of being less than a gentleman would only bring censure down upon your own head."

She stared into his eyes, her breath coming rapidly. "But why? Why would a man of his ilk even be included in a genteel entertainment such as this? No, my lord, I must tell Louisa at once what a scurrilous dog Lord Davies is."

"My dear landlady, you are an intelligent girl, but naive when it comes to the ways of Society. Lord Davies comes from an excellent family. He is a baron. He desires to be considered a Dandy, true, but he has brought no scandal to his name yet. Therefore, he is accepted."

She appeared to consider this. "Very well, I shall speak to my sister later this evening." Her voice trembled slightly as she said, "I love her, you see, and it is my duty to lead her mind down a virtuous path. Now, please, your position on this bench is indecorous."

The marquess grinned mischievously. More than ever, he wished to further their association. "Do you agree to be guided by me in your quest to bring Mr. Sedgewick up to scratch?"

"Am I to understand you will not release me until I give you what you want?"

Lord Carrisworth's voice dropped to a husky whisper. "You could hardly do that on this uncomfortable bench in the middle of a party."

Miss Pymbroke briefly raised her eyes to the heavens. Then, turning to face him, the thought suddenly occurred to her that he merely wished to tease her. That if she were

to respond to his advances—which she never would!—
he would draw back.

But she quickly dismissed this theory as foolish.

She sighed heavily and her face took on a self-righteous
expression. "Perhaps *I* am meant to guide *you*, my lord.
Yes, I shall accept your help, and mayhap you will learn
more proper behavior in the process. Have you sent those
two French girls away yet?"

The marquess sat back on the bench and laughed
aloud.

Chapter Five

After Lord Carrisworth returned the ladies to South Audley Street and took his leave, Louisa went directly to her bedchamber.

Verity began climbing the stairs behind her, meaning to have that much-desired talk with her sister, when Lady Iris summoned her to the drawing room.

Lady Hyacinth was already seated on the dark blue settee. She spoke as Verity and Lady Iris settled themselves in nearby chairs. "Was it not a delightful afternoon? If the delicacies we were treated to are any indication, I can only imagine Lady Foxworth keeps a French chef."

Casting her sister an arch look, Lady Hyacinth continued in a voice full of meaning, " 'Tis a pity we do not have a French chef. Perhaps if Iris were not such a pinch penny . . ."

Lady Iris's gaze ran over her sister's plump figure. "If you ate some Frenchie's cooking every day, England would soon sink into the Atlantic under the weight of you!"

"At least *I* shall never have to resort to wearing false breasts," Lady Hyacinth retorted, puffing out her ample bosom while staring accusingly at the swells of wrinkled flesh emerging from Lady Iris's old-fashioned gown.

"Fiend seize it!" Lady Iris screamed. She reached into the bodice of her dress, pulled out two rounded wax pads, and hurled them at her sister's head.

From long practice, Lady Hyacinth successfully dodged these indelicate articles, smiling victoriously at having once again goaded her sister into one of her displays of temper.

Verity held back a laugh. Since coming to live with the ladies, she had realized that underneath their frequent bickering they held a deep affection for each other. Indeed, how dull their lives would be if they did not have one another with whom to brangle.

These thoughts filled Verity with an urgency to be on her way upstairs to see her own sister. "Lady Iris, was there something you wished to speak to me about?"

"Yes, gel," Lady Iris replied, turning to look at her. "I have good news. I approached Lady Sefton as she was leaving the Foxworths', and she kindly consented to send you vouchers to Almack's."

Lady Hyacinth gasped in delight. "Only the best gentlemen are allowed there, dear child, and while the refreshments are deplorable, one might dance the evening away with several handsome young gallants."

Verity's eyes shone. "Naturally I know of Almack's. I confess I have often wondered what it might be like to go there. I am certain, since the cream of Society attend, the people are most kind and virtuous."

"Hmph," Lady Iris snorted at this gross piece of naiveté. "We'll go to the ball Wednesday next."

"Oh, I must tell Louisa. She will be so excited," Verity exclaimed, rising.

Lady Iris swiftly put a stop to this plan. "Verity! I said *you* have been extended vouchers. Louisa has not."

Verity whirled from the doorway, her expression dismayed. "Why?"

Lady Iris and Lady Hyacinth exchanged significant glances.

"The patronesses of Almack's are notoriously high in the instep," Lady Hyacinth said gently.

"What can that signify? If they have approved me, they must approve Louisa. We are both the daughters of a viscount."

"I did not ask Lady Sefton why Louisa may not be admitted," Lady Iris said, knowing full well that whispers of Louisa's shameful behavior on the continent had reached the ears of the powerful patronesses. "You must not concern yourself with the matter. Louisa will be able to amuse herself in our absence Wednesday night."

Verity threw back her head in her martyred way. "How differently we feel, my lady. It most certainly is my concern that my sister has been slighted. I should never consider going to a place she was not welcome."

Lady Iris leaned forward in her chair. "Come down off your high ropes, gel. It is all well and good for you to show concern for Louisa, but do not think you can make her into something she is not."

Verity raised her chin. "I love my sister and shall show my loyalty to her by not attending Almack's." She quickly left the room.

"Foolish chit. All that loyalty is misplaced and likely to land her in a scrape," Lady Iris declared. Then she muttered, "Ah, well, Carrisworth never bothers with the place anyway. Too many young misses trying to trap a husband."

Lady Hyacinth leaned forward and whispered, "Iris,

you've had the same thought as I. The marquess and Verity. Nothing could be more suitable."

Lady Iris scowled. "I had that thought long before you did, Sister. And I'll thank you to guard your tongue about it. 'Twould not do for Carrisworth to know our plans are for him to be a tenant-for-life!"

The object of the sisters' matchmaking lounged in White's. Although Lord Carrisworth had been drinking steadily since his arrival, he was merely feeling merry and was engaged in a lively discussion of a wager newly entered in White's betting book. Sir Joseph Copley had bet Mr. Blackford fifty guineas that Bonaparte would not be alive on this day three years hence.

"I should not involve myself in such a wager, Perry," a familiar voice said close to the marquess's ear. "A wiser gamble might be that Napoleon would not still be emperor in three years."

His lordship slowly twisted round in his chair and saw his old friend, Charles, the Earl of Northbridge. "Charles, can it be you? I thought you were buried in the country with your new bride."

Lord Northbridge was a good-natured, attractive man of average height. His brown hair held a hint of gray at the temples, and he had a network of lines around his eyes from smiling, which he did often.

"Jealous, are you, Perry? Wish you had a wife yourself? I arrived in Town less than a week ago, and all I have heard are tales of your wicked ways with the ladies. Really, my friend, *twins*?"

Grinning, Lord Carrisworth rose to his feet and shook the earl's outstretched hand. Then, he clapped his old friend on the back, saying, "Damned good to see you, Charles. How is Cynthia?"

The two men moved away to a private table where they seated themselves and ordered brandy.

"Hah!" Lord Northbridge responded. "I believe what you really want to know is what has kept me from Town so long. Well, it is like this. Excellent—that is what I have taken to calling Cynthia because it is an apt nickname—and I traveled quite a bit after the wedding. Last fall, we arrived at my estate and have spent our time putting things in order. She shares my interest in ancient pottery, the darling girl. But, we were both ready for a little fun in Town, and what better time than the Season?"

"Ancient pottery?" The marquess scoffed. He waved the waiter away, raised his glass, and quickly swallowed some brandy. "I am glad to see you, Charles, but I suppose things will not be the same now that you have been caught in the parson's mousetrap. No more late nights, no more competing over bits of muslin."

Lord Northbridge let out a booming laugh. "I never could compete against you with the muslin set, Perry. Except I must say you did not have a chance with Excellent."

"True," Lord Carrisworth said casually. "In you she saw a rake she could reform. In me she saw a self-indulgent *débauché*. Will you attend the masquerade tomorrow night in Portman Square?"

The earl's brows came together. "That is predicted to be a wild affair. It is true, then, you are not ready to settle down. Take it from me, Perry, the married state is much maligned. I have never been happier in my life. Can you say the same?"

The Marquess of Carrisworth rose languidly to his feet. "Your waistline looks content, Charles, and I am pleased you are satisfied with Cynthia. But do not look to me to follow your example. I shall never marry."

Lord Northbridge watched his friend make his way out of the club. He noted the marquess had not answered his question regarding his state of happiness.

But then, the answer was plain to anyone who had known Perry as long as he had. He remembered how Perry had always come home with him for holidays while they were at Oxford. The boy never wanted to go to his own family. Something about his mother.

The earl sipped his brandy. Oh, the mischief they had contrived to get into during those breaks from school! Later, they had been two young bucks on the town getting into all the usual scrapes.

He had grown out of all that. But Perry seemed to have sunk further into the depths of pleasure-seeking. Not that Lord Northbridge believed this nonsensical story about Perry having a set of twins in keeping. There was more to it than that, he'd wager. Perhaps he had arrived on the scene just in time to save his friend from himself.

The earl drained his glass. It was late. Excellent would be waiting for him. A large smile creased his face. Perry's problems could wait.

The next night Verity sat alone over a tea tray. The Ladies Iris and Hyacinth had been engaged for an evening of whist with friends. Verity had declined the sisters' offer to include her in the party, informing them she did not approve of card playing, feeling it could lead to the more dangerous practice of gambling.

Lady Iris had pooh-poohed this theory, declaring all genteel ladies indulged in harmless card parties. Lady Hyacinth had added her entreaties saying, "There is bound to be a delicious array of cakes, tarts, and pastries as Lady Edwina is monstrously addicted to sweets," but Verity could not be swayed in her convictions. The frustrated sisters had left the house without her.

Reaching down to pour herself a final cup of tea before retiring to her room to read, Verity's hand brushed Empress's fluffy tail. "Well, my girl, 'tis only you and me. The ladies are out, and Louisa is in bed with the headache."

Empress's tail twitched. She watched Verity drink from the teacup and miaowed pathetically.

Verity chuckled and poured out a small measure of cream for the regal cat as she had seen Lady Iris do on occasion. She placed the dish on the floor and observed the animal's pink tongue daintily, but thoroughly, lapping the treat.

"There, that tastes better than that dreadful mouse you laid on Louisa's pillow, does it not, you naughty puss?"

Empress paused for a brief second to cast a rueful glance upon her benefactress.

"Very well, I shall not tease you about it, as I see you realize it is not seemly for a cat of your consequence to play such tricks."

As if in agreement, Empress miaowed with a mouth full of cream. Finishing up, she began the arduous task of washing. She licked her left paw meticulously, then used it to clean the area around her left eye below her crown of white fur.

Verity sighed heavily. "If only my sister would agree as easily with my notions of what is proper behavior. Last night when I spoke with her, ever so tactfully, about her use of cosmetics she laughed at me. When I went on to insist her conduct with Sir Ramsey and Lord Davies was not at all the thing, she pronounced me a prude and an . . . an unnatural sister."

"I left Louisa my copy of *Christian Thoughts* and can only hope reading it will help her." Tears formed in Verity's eyes, but she dashed them away quickly. "I do want to help, you know, Empress," she whispered.

The cat's paw froze in midair while she watched the girl.

Composing herself, Verity said, "I am for bed. Come, you may stay with me until Lady Iris returns."

The animal followed her upstairs, pausing outside Louisa's bedchamber. She reached a tentative paw up toward the doorknob.

"No, no, Empress, this way," Verity called.

The cat stood stubbornly where she was. "Miaow!"

On impulse, Verity knocked softly on Louisa's door. Receiving no response, she entered the room. "Louisa, dear, are you feeling better?"

Verity held her candle high and saw the room was empty. With a little start of fear, she rang the bell. Moments later, Betty appeared in the doorway.

"Where is Mrs. Barrington, Betty?"

Betty looked down at the floor. "I'm not supposed to say."

"What can you mean?" Verity cried. "Tell me at once where my sister is."

The maid threw her apron over her head in a paroxysm of weeping. "Oh, miss, she told me I'd lose my place . . ."

"Nonsense. Think, Betty, I am your employer, and your position is secure. That is, unless you continue to refuse to answer my question."

Betty lowered the apron. "Mrs. Barrington left the house without you knowin' to go to a masked ball with Sir Ramsey," Betty wailed. "She knew you wouldn't approve and didn't want you to try to stop her."

Verity gasped in alarm. "A masked ball! Good heavens." Her mind raced. Cecil Sedgewick had, without going into details, once mentioned that such affairs often turned into romps. Surely Louisa did not know what perils awaited her. She, Verity, would have to go after her sister and see her safely home.

"Betty, did Mrs. Barrington say where the ball was being held?"

"Yes, miss. In Portman Square." Perceiving her mistress's intention, the maid so far forgot herself to exclaim, "Never say you are goin' to fetch her!"

"I most certainly am, and you are going with me." Ignoring the maid's frightened face, Verity said, "I do not want to attract any undue attention. I shall need a gown and a domino."

The maid reluctantly went to the armoire that held Louisa's wardrobe. Verity quickly decided on a laurel pink ballgown, and Betty found a white velvet domino with a matching mask.

"Run downstairs, Betty, and hail a hack, then come help me finish dressing."

With trembling fingers, Verity stripped off her old gray dress, reflecting that only that morning she had been next door peacefully working in her garden. She had not known whether to be sorry or glad when she had not seen the disturbing marquess.

A wayward thought flashed across her frenzied brain. What would he think if he knew she was rushing off to such a nefarious entertainment? Alas, the wretch would probably give his wholehearted approval.

Verity did not know the number of the house where the masquerade was being held. She therefore instructed the driver of the hackney coach to drive around Portman Square until told to halt.

Betty sat huddled nervously in the corner of the coach. "Miss, please, let's go home. I'm that sure Mrs. Barrington can take care of herself."

Her attention on the passing houses, Verity said, "I am persuaded she does not know the wickedness of this party. Such want of caution is not to be desired, but is understandable in someone with Louisa's high spirits."

"But, miss, you haring off like this without a gentleman to protect you ain't right either," Betty protested.

"Hush, Betty," Verity ordered in the face of this truth. "You are impertinent." Then she spied a couple dressed as Sir Walter Raleigh and Queen Elizabeth hurrying up a walkway and being admitted to a gray stone house. She quickly lowered the glass and called to the coachman to stop.

After alighting from the vehicle and paying the driver, Verity and Betty stood alone on the chilly street. Verity looked up at the house, a shiver of apprehension stopping her from proceeding to the door.

Usually, during an entertainment, the hostess would be sure all the draperies of the house were pulled back and numerous candles lit, so passersby could look enviously upon all the finely dressed ladies and gentlemen gracing her home.

However, all the curtains of this house were drawn tightly against curious eyes. Muted sounds of laughter could be heard coming from within.

Ignoring her feelings of trepidation, Verity straightened her shoulders, adjusted her mask, and marched toward the door, the white velvet domino flowing out behind her. Betty followed, muttering of dire happenings sure to befall them.

Their knock was answered immediately, not by a butler, but by a court jester who waved them inside with drunken exuberance.

Verity crossed into the hallway, her brown eyes widening as she took in her surroundings.

The rooms were crowded with people dressed in everything from elaborate costumes to formal ball dress with only a mask to conceal their identity. Everyone appeared very lively. Most seemed to be drinking heavily and feeling the effects. Verity felt heat rush to her face as she realized many of the ladies were wearing near-transparent dresses. Some of the men danced with *both* arms around their partners.

She experienced a strong desire to turn and run back out the door. If only she could find Louisa and Sir Ramsey.

A mere few feet away on the other side of a Greek statue, Louisa stood staring at the girl who had just entered the room. She did not recognize her sister by her face, but rather by her own pink gown and white domino. Grinding her teeth in frustration, Louisa realized her prudish little sister had found her out and would shortly spoil her evening.

She turned to Sir Ramsey, her gray eyes beseeching him from under her lashes. "La, sir, I fear I grow weary of this ball. After that boring breakfast at the Foxworths', you promised me some fun. Perhaps you know of a quiet place we could go, where we might be allowed some privacy."

Staring down at Mrs. Barrington's nipples, which were revealed through her filmy white Roman gown, Sir Ramsey's face broke into a smile. They could be quite alone at his townhouse. And the lady was most willing. "I know just the place."

Verity did not notice them when they slipped past her out the front door. She did perceive that Betty, who had become more distraught with each passing minute, had become separated from her in the crush, but she refused to let her maid's disappearance distract her from the task at hand.

Suddenly her thoughts focused on her own safety when a young man in a gypsy costume dared to place his arms around her waist and dance her halfway around the room before she could stop him. Verity began giving him a blistering set-down.

Several people surrounding the pair heard the lady's tone and moralizing lecture, and a laughing group gathered around them goading the young man to take further liberties.

Across the room, the Marquess of Carrisworth, striking in evening clothes and a black mask, was trying to detach himself from his former mistress. Roxanna had clung to him since his arrival at the masquerade some thirty minutes before. While she was magnificent in a revealing costume meant to represent Venus, he received the distinct impression she was trying to lure him back to her bed.

Really, he thought with some irritation, he was done with her and she should know it. Idly, he wondered what all the fuss was about on the other side of the room. He decided to use whatever it was as an excuse to be rid of her. "Roxanna, you know I have an insatiable curiosity. I am intrigued by that fracas. Excuse me while I investigate."

Leaving the thwarted Roxanna behind, he sauntered through the crowd.

In the middle of the jeering circle of faces, Verity felt small and alone. Then her gaze fell on a man dressed in clerical garb holding a Bible and peering at her intently. She fell upon him like an anchor in a storm.

"Oh, sir, have you come to save these corrupt souls? I, too, feel it my duty to help the wicked see the light," she cried out in a ringing voice, deliriously happy now that it appeared rescue was at hand.

Her relief was short lived.

"Corruption of souls is indeed why I am here," the "preacher" intoned. Then, without warning, he grabbed her and pulled her flush against him. With one hand he held her tight, while his other hand moved to rip open the front of her domino, revealing her dress. He then grasped her chin in a fierce hold. The crowd called out their encouragements.

Verity opened her mouth and screamed. Immediately, she felt the lecherous preacher torn from her, and she stumbled to the floor from the suddenness of the movement.

Verity heard the fickle crowd now cheering a tall gentleman in evening dress who she saw was delivering a crushing blow to the preacher's jaw. The Bible went flying, and the preacher was stretched out unconscious on the floor.

The ball was rapidly disintegrating into a romp. Trying to rise to her feet, Verity abruptly felt herself lifted up into the tall gentleman's arms and carried out the front door of the house amidst more whistles and cheers. Out on the street, she struggled against him, fearing yet another attack on her person.

"Ouch! Be still, you little minx."

Verity froze. For the first time she looked up into the

green eyes glaring at her from behind the black mask. "Oh," she exclaimed resentfully. "It is you!"

"Is that the thanks I get for freeing you from that 'preacher,' Miss Pymbroke?" Lord Carrisworth queried. "By God, I should have left you. Now that I think on it, I recall you are immensely attracted to members of the clergy."

His face was so close to her own, Verity found her breath coming in gasps. "Release me at once, my lord."

The marquess obliged her by dropping her unceremoniously to her feet. "Are you going to run back inside and exchange sermons with that imposter?"

Ignoring this mocking question, Verity asked, "How did you recognize me?"

Lord Carrisworth threw back his dark head and laughed. "Who else would be standing in the middle of a masquerade delivering a jaw-me-dead? What in heaven's name were you doing there in the first place?"

Remembering her sister's plight, Verity's hands flew to her cheeks. "Oh, my lord, my sister is in there. I must find her and take her home."

She turned as if to go back. Lord Carrisworth reached out his arm and spun her around on her heel. His gaze dropped to the neck of her gown. The pink dress was tight across her bosom, pushing the two ivory mounds of her breasts up against the cloth. The marquess tore his gaze from the tantalizing sight. "There is no need. Mrs. Barrington left with Sir Ramsey about twenty minutes ago."

"She did? Thank goodness she is safe."

The marquess kept his thoughts to himself. He judged it would not be prudent to inform Miss Pymbroke that her sister was at that very moment most likely in Sir Ramsey's bed.

Verity looked at him curiously. "What were you doing in such low company, my lord? I could tell from the inelegant speech of some of the guests I was not in Polite Society. Why would someone of your rank attend ..." she trailed off, seeing the cynical amusement in his eyes. She turned her head away.

Perceiving the disapproval in her posture, the marquess paused. He had truly not been enjoying the evening. It could only have ended in another meaningless flirtation, like so many he had enjoyed in the past, the thought of which now brought no anticipation of pleasure.

He noticed she was shivering. "Come now, you cannot be cold, my avenging angel. Surely, the mantle of virtue you always cloak yourself in will keep you warm."

She turned to him, a sudden flash of insight making her respond tartly. "Just as the reputation of a dissolute rake keeps you from any real feelings, my lord?"

The marquess felt like shaking her. Instead, he decided to be shot of her as quickly as possible. "Miss Pymbroke, allow me to escort you home. I have my Town coach." He signaled to a servant a short distance down the street, and a moment later a vehicle pulled up in front of them.

She laid a small hand on his arm. "My lord, I almost forgot. My maid, Betty, was with me, and I do not know what happened to her."

Lord Carrisworth released his breath in a long-suffering sigh. "Stay here with my servant until I return. Indeed, get in the coach and wait for me."

Verity pursed her lips. "I shall not. It is a closed carriage, and the rules of what is proper behavior for an unmarried lady state she must not ride in a closed carriage alone with a gentleman."

"Good God, was there *ever* such a female? Miss Pymbroke, since we determined at the Foxworths' breakfast yesterday that I am no *gentleman*, it cannot signify. Now, get in the coach, and hopefully I shall return in a few minutes with Betty."

"Jake," he called to the coachman. "Look after the lady." He strode off toward the house without so much as a backward glance.

Verity stood by the vehicle, half in anticipation, half in dread. Where was Betty? Had she been frightened enough by the goings on to leave?

Most disturbing, though, was the thought of being alone with the marquess. The strength of his arms around her when he had carried her out of the house had been exhilarating.

Verity bit her lip. The night air was growing colder. How else was she to get home if she did not accept his offer of transport? She had been in such a rush to leave the house, she had failed to bring sufficient coins with her for another hack.

The marquess's servant was standing at attention, the door to the coach open. Making up her mind, Verity accepted his hand and entered the coach.

She loosened the white domino, then reached up and untied the strings of the mask, allowing the hood to fall back.

A moment later, she jumped when the door to the coach opened, and the marquess entered, his tall body suddenly making the roomy coach seem small.

They were very much alone.

Instead of taking the seat opposite her, his lordship sat beside Verity, forcing her to move over. He gave the order to the coachman for home, then, untying his mask, said softly, "It seems your heartless maid was last seen running headlong into the night soon after your arrival."

Verity found she could not muster much concern for Betty. She stared at the gentleman beside her and noticed the strength of his long, white fingers. In the closeness of the coach, she could smell the faint lime scent he always wore.

She turned her head abruptly away.

The marquess studied her profile. God, she was beautiful. Did she not realize the effect that too-tight pink gown would have on a man?

And her eyes. They reflected her feelings so well. They sparkled when she was angry. They softened when they rested on someone she cared for. They shed tears when her heart was touched, such as during the play.

And they avoided him when he made her uncomfortable. Like now. He did not want her to avoid him, he thought unexpectedly.

"Come, Miss Pymbroke. Would I take advantage of a moment like this? Use it for my own evil intentions?"

This was said in such a mocking manner, Verity could only stare at the skirt of her gown, all the while hiding a blush.

Abruptly, without quite knowing how it happened, she found herself across the marquess's lap. She barely had time to look up into his laughing eyes before he murmured, "You know me so well," and his lips came down on hers.

Verity had never been kissed before. The touch of the marquess's lips on her mouth set her body aflame. All at once her rules flew out the window, and she could not get enough of his warm, firm lips. She returned his kiss with reckless abandon, shutting out any emotions save the ones he was calling forth. In response, she heard a low moan come from the marquess's throat, which only served to heighten her passion.

Then, somewhere in the distance, Verity could hear church bells ring. Abruptly, she was hurtled back to the reality that she was kissing the Marquess of Carrisworth, a known rake.

She tore herself out of his arms, her breath coming hard and fast. His lordship's eyes were heavy lidded and half closed. She could see his lips were still moist from their kiss.

Stung by her withdrawal, the marquess drawled, "I *beg* your pardon."

Verity began to shake. This, then, was what came from ignoring the conventions, from breaking rules.

The coach had come to a stop in South Audley Street. Without a word, Verity scrambled out and ran up the steps to Lady Iris's.

Lord Carrisworth deemed it necessary to remain where he was for a minute for decency's sake.

For the first time, he judged he had been less than clever with a lady. Miss Pymbroke's innocence struck him like a reproach.

The marquess tried to relax, leaning his dark head back against the comfortable leather squabs of the seat. What a fool he was! How did the old saying go? "Be Careful What You Wish Lest You Get It"?

He had wanted to see if a passionate nature lay beneath Miss Pymbroke's outwardly prim behavior. Now he had gotten his wish and had his answer.

What he had not counted on was his own response.

Devil take it! Perhaps an hour with one of the twins *was* what it was going to take to banish the memory of a pair of the sweetest lips he had ever tasted.

"Devil take all virgins," he said under his breath. Then he shouted to the coachman, "Take me to Half Moon Street, Jake."

Chapter Six

For the second time in as many months, Lord Carrisworth stood in Rundell and Bridge's, gazing down at a dazzling array of diamond necklaces that had been brought out for his inspection. On this occasion, he needed two of the expensive baubles.

His mind went back to the night before. That particular part of his anatomy eager for action when Miss Pymbroke had been in the carriage had seemed to have dosed itself with laudanum between South Audley Street and the twins' residence in Half Moon Street.

It was just as well. By the time he was ensconced in their sitting room listening to their chatter, he'd realized the folly of thinking one of them could satisfy his desire for Miss Pymbroke.

The visit had proven worthwhile, however. Monique and Dominique's popularity on the stage had grown to remarkable proportions. The marquess had talked with them about the future, then outlined a plan. It would enable them to live on their earnings, along with a generous settlement from him, all of which would be carefully invested and looked after by his own competent solicitor. The girls' happiness prompted them to kiss his lordship's cheek declaring he was better to them than their own Papa. This, of course, caused the marquess to stoutly admonish them never to repeat those words in Society.

Soon after arising the next morn, Lord Carrisworth decided it would be prudent to visit the famous jewelers in order to obtain the gifts that would publicly signal their dismissal as his "mistresses."

Deliberating over his selection, he heard the door to the shop open. "Perry!" the Earl of Northbridge called out. "You are looking grave as a judge. Have you decided on a bride after all? One who finds the family betrothal ring not to her taste?"

The marquess grinned. "How ridiculous. I should not wish to enter an institution which has so obviously addled your wits. I am here purchasing Monique and Dominique's farewell jewels. Why are you here? Selecting a trinket for a new flirt?"

Lord Northbridge's face rapidly lost its smile. His expression serious, he spoke quietly. "Cynthia and I will be celebrating the anniversary of the night she agreed to become my wife. I have come to commission something special."

The marquess raised a long-fingered hand to his brow. "Damn my tongue. Accept my apologies, Charles? I am weak of brain this morning."

Never one to remain vexed for long, the earl clapped his friend on the back. "I shall forgive you on the condition you accompany Cynthia and me to the Lexhams' turtle dinner tonight."

"The Lexhams? Such exemplary company. Too tedious by half," the marquess grumbled. Seeing the stubborn look in the earl's eye, however, he capitulated. "Very well, Charles. Since I am shortly to be mistress-less and have no other plans for the evening."

The two gentlemen decided on a meeting time and

parted company amiably when the earl moved down the counter to consult with one of the jewelers.

Selecting two necklaces at random, Lord Carrisworth scribbled out the twins' direction and concluded his transaction. He began turning away from the counter only to have his attention caught by a shimmering set of yellow topaz eardrops.

Immediately, a picture formed in his mind of the golden highlights that graced Miss Pymbroke's brown tresses. The eardrops would complement her coloring perfectly. Of course, she would refuse such a gift as improper. Gentlemen restricted their tokens for the ladies to something inconsequential like flowers or sweetmeats. He could not give them to her.

Noticing his interest, the man behind the counter swiftly said, "You have superb taste, my lord. Those are particularly fine stones from India."

The eardrops winked up at him.

It was then Lord Carrisworth remembered he rarely behaved like a proper gentleman. "Wrap them up," he commanded.

Kitchen maid Molly Grimes hurried through the windy London streets on an urgent errand. She ran because Mrs. Witherspoon, the cook who ruled her domain with a heavy skillet, would box her ears if she dawdled. Lady Lexham was holding a turtle dinner that very night, and Mrs. Witherspoon had been horrified when she found they were short of the necessary bay leaves for the turtle soup.

Breathless, Molly entered a shop with *Jack Millweed, Apothecary and Herbalist* inscribed above the door. Her heart sank when she saw the proprietor was busy with another customer.

Ten agonizing minutes went by without Mr. Millweed being able to serve her. Growing more frightened as every minute passed, Molly finally screwed up her courage and called to a girl engaged in dusting the bottles behind the counter. "Please, miss, could you 'elp me? I'll be in terrible trouble if I don't get back soon."

Lizzie Millweed glanced at her father and received a nod of consent. "My name's Lizzie. What can I get you?"

Gratefully, Molly gave her order and began chatting. She was in awe of all the herbs and potions around her. A good country girl, she believed the mysterious powers of the elixirs could cure anything.

As Lizzie handed her the bay leaves and two pence change, Molly lowered her voice to a whisper. "There be a 'andsome first footman I've wanted to walk out with for ever so long. Do you 'ave any love potion I could get with this 'ere money?"

Lizzie looked doubtfully at the coins. Then, her expression brightened. She leaned close to Molly and said, "I can get you something, but don't tell no one. Some gentry-mort paid for it, then ordered it thrown out."

Both girls rolled their eyes at the strange ways of the Quality.

Lizzie disappeared into the back room for a moment. When she returned, she darted a furtive glance at her father before slipping Molly a bottle marked "Love's Helping Hand." Molly couldn't read, but Lizzie giggled and assured her it would make whoever took it nice and friendly.

After thanking her, Molly ran all the way back to Lady Lexham's, but still received a sharp slap from Mrs. Witherspoon, who declared she had taken too long.

Rubbing her reddened cheek, Molly covertly watched the cook add the bay leaves to a large pot of simmering turtle soup. She knew Mrs. Witherspoon would be tasting the soup throughout the day.

As soon as the older woman bustled away, Molly ran to the pot and poured in half the contents of the bottle Lizzie had given her. Had not Lizzie said it would turn anyone nice? And she still had plenty left for Will, the footman.

Despite her throbbing cheek, Molly went about her duties humming.

Clad in a blue sprigged morning gown, Verity sat in the window seat of her bedchamber, gazing down at South Audley Street. More than once she had told herself she was not hoping to catch a glimpse of the Marquess of Carrisworth. She was merely admiring the fine day and organizing her somewhat troubled thoughts.

"Here is that sanctimonious book you left for me, Mouse," Louisa said, sweeping into the room and handing Verity the copy of *Christian Thoughts*. "I do wish you would refrain from preaching to me, and that includes giving me sermonizing books."

Turning her gaze to her sister, Verity said, "I do not look at it as 'preaching.' " She placed the book next to her and held out her hands to Louisa. "Dear Louisa, it is only out of my affection for you that I beg you to think how easily one's reputation is damaged. I know you told me at breakfast that you left that shameful masked ball well before it grew wild, but to attend it to begin with was surely unwise."

"Pooh," Louisa scoffed, ignoring Verity's outstretched hands and instead studying her reflection in the glass above the satinwood dressing table. "You forget, as a widow I am allowed much more freedom than you."

Verity dropped her hands to her sides. "Even so, people will gossip."

Apparently satisfied with her appearance, Louisa turned a speculative gaze toward her sister. "Your own reputation would be damaged far more than mine if word got out that *you* had appeared in Portman Square last night, so let us not speak of it again. I am going driving with Sir Ramsey—no, don't say a word against him. Someone must amuse me today since Lady Iris has insisted on dragging us all to Lady Lexham's dull turtle dinner tonight."

Louisa blew Verity a careless kiss and tripped from the room.

Verity sighed and shrugged her shoulders. For the moment, she could not concern herself with Louisa's behavior. It was her own mortifying actions of the night before that had served to bring hot color to her face every time she remembered them.

And she had been able to do little that morning save recall her response to Lord Carrisworth's disturbing kiss. Wanton! That is what she had been. And, further, there was the humiliating fact that whenever she thought of her reaction, by necessity she relived every moment of his embrace.

As the image focused in her memory, she could see again the laughter in his green eyes before his lips came down on hers. She closed her eyes and remembered the potent sensations that had flooded her body at the warm touch of his mouth and the strong feel of his arms around her. Her lips tingled at the memory.

Verity pressed shaking fingers to her mouth. This would not do! Ladies did not have lustful notions. She picked up the copy of *Christian Thoughts* and held it to her as if it would shield her from her own thoughts and feelings. She was foolish beyond permission for allowing the practiced charms of a rake to affect her so. Drawing a deep breath, she determined to be on full guard around the marquess, lest she end as just another of his amusements—like the twins

A scratching on the door preceded the entrance of a meek Betty. "Lord Davies has called to see you, miss."

Good Heavens! Verity thought. What on earth could he want? "Show him into the drawing room. I shall be down presently. And, Betty, there is no need to take yourself to task any longer about last night. You explained your fears to me and said you were sorry for your actions." The maid's tearful apology earlier had touched Verity's heart. "Let us forget the matter."

Betty straightened her shoulders. "Thank you, miss."

Downstairs a few minutes later, ensconced in the drawing room, Lord Davies stood admiring himself in the pier glass. With his new false calves providing his legs with an athletic build, his lavender pantaloons looked very fine indeed. A pink- and lavender-striped waistcoat, topped by a plum-colored coat, nipped in at the waist and well padded at the shoulders, completed his ensemble.

Despite his pleasure in his appearance, Lord Davies chewed his fingernail nervously. Roxanna Hollings had given him this assignment, for which she was prepared to pay him handsomely.

The actress had summoned the baron to her house the day before, and after seeing him comfortably seated with a glass of the best canary had proposed her plan. "I have a mind to be Carrisworth's mistress again, James. The respect I command as such pleases me. I do not view those silly French girls as any obstacle. Rather I am convinced his thoughts are taken up by that moralizing

Miss *Prim*broke." Roxanna's red lips formed a moue of distaste.

Lord Davies said, "Very pretty girl, Miss Pymbroke. Innocent-like and refreshing. Her Puritan airs add to her charm."

Roxanna's blue eyes narrowed. "Men are contrary, and if you tell them they can't have something, they immediately decide it is the only thing they want. The Pymbroke chit is forbidden fruit, and since there is nothing more appealing to a man of the world"—Roxanna snapped her fingers for emphasis—"his interest is captured."

Lord Davies's brow furrowed, but he immediately smoothed it with his fingertips, fearing the formation of a wrinkle. "So you've been plotting. What do you want me to do?"

As she considered him, Roxanna's lips curved into a smile. "Ah, James, it is unfortunate you cannot be as perceptive at the gaming tables."

Ignoring the ugly flush that rose to his lordship's face, she continued. "If Carrisworth were to see the virtuous Miss Pymbroke giving you her warmest attentions, he would believe she is just like any other female and some of her luster would fade."

"But she's already rejected me once. You saw for yourself, the afternoon at the theater," Lord Davies protested.

"True. But you were too blunt. You must win her trust, then carry out the plan."

Lord Davies's expression suddenly turned shrewd. "What's in it for me?"

Roxanna rose and poured out another measure of wine for her guest. "My new protector, Rupert, the Duke of Covington, is rich as Croesus. I shall supply you with money for your penchant for gaming . . . and, if all goes well, perhaps even pay off your tailor as a bonus," she ended with a chuckle.

Lord Davies was once a wealthy man, but deep gambling, resulting in heavy losses, and an obsession for clothes had finally reduced him to being purse-pinched. News of this had reached his tailor, making that merchant increasingly reluctant to extend the baron any further credit.

At the thought of his debts being wiped away and his tailor's willingness to supply him with whatever he desired, Lord Davies's pulses quickened as they never had under the ministrations of any female, no matter how desirable. He licked his lips. "I'll do it," he told the pleased Roxanna.

Now, in South Audley Street, Miss Pymbroke entered the drawing room, dropped him a brief curtsy and, with a coldly questioning look, settled herself in a chair. Lord Davies charged forward with his scheme to ingratiate himself with the straitlaced young girl.

"Miss Pymbroke," he cried in a voice full of anguish. He dropped to one knee in front of her, at the last moment adroitly placing a handkerchief on the floor so as not to soil his lavender pantaloons. "I am deeply ashamed of my boorish behavior toward you at the theater. Say you forgive me and smile upon me, else I shall shoot myself!"

"Lord Davies!" Verity exclaimed, startled by his dramatic assertion. "Do not speak so, I pray you. Please, sit down and calm yourself."

"Nay!" Lord Davies declared, throwing himself into his role for all he was worth. "My life is meaningless. I have no morals to guide me and have offended a lady whose beliefs make her so high above me I am not deserving of kissing the hem of her gown."

A bubble of laughter formed in Verity's throat. With Lord Davies's chubby cheeks and his bushy red hair, he reminded her more than ever of a red squirrel, especially in his present position, kneeling in front of her as if he were begging for a particularly tasty nut. She cast a quick look of reproach at Betty, seated in the corner of the room for propriety, who had not been able to suppress a giggle.

Turning her attention back to Lord Davies, Verity said, "My lord, I repeat, please sit down. You may be at your ease while we discuss this. I am willing to forgive you for your actions in the Green Room if you are truly sorry."

Lord Davies moved to the dark blue settee. He did not notice when Empress padded into the room and soundlessly vaulted to the back of the settee.

"Indeed, I am truly repentant, but, Miss Pymbroke, you see before you a man lost in a sea of confusion," he said earnestly.

Verity was only half listening to him. Her gaze was caught by Empress, whose feline face was a study in curiosity. The cat moved forward and raised a silver-colored paw above Lord Davies's head. She patted the top of his wiry hair, perhaps in an effort to discover what it was.

His lordship turned round sharply. "Be gone!"

The offended cat jumped to the floor.

"Ahem, as I was saying, Miss Pymbroke, I beg you to instruct me onto a more virtuous path."

"My lord, it is always beneficial when one sees room for improvement in one's character, but I fail to comprehend what I can do for you."

Lord Davies leaned forward eagerly. "If you could but spare me of your time to further my education . . ."

Again, Verity could barely concentrate on his reply because Empress, now creeping out from under the settee, was stalking the baron's Hessian boots. With alarm, she thought the tassels might be as tempting to the cat as the beloved ribbons.

"I plead for your guidance," Lord Davies went on.

Before Verity could utter a warning, one lightning quick paw reached out to the closest tassel and sharp claws ripped it from its mooring. The delighted cat took her prize and batted it across the floor, happily engaged in a game of toss, chase, and capture.

Lord Davies's eyes popped at the sight. Reaching down to his scratched boot, he uttered a strangled sound and turned pale.

"Empress! You . . . naughty . . . cat," Verity gasped. But the situation was too much for her, and she collapsed into laughter.

Lord Davies's face grew as red as his hair while he choked back his fury. Then, he made a swift recovery. Seizing the moment he managed an artificial chuckle. "You see, Miss Pymbroke, what a good influence you are on me? Why, only yesterday I might have scolded that dear little kitty for such an action. While now, in your presence, I find myself tranquil in mind and able to accept the loss of my boot as no great concern. Won't you agree to educate me so all my thoughts can be so admirable?"

Although part of Verity's brain viewed the dandy's proclamation disbelievingly, her moral character could not refuse what might be a genuine plea for help. "Very well, Lord Davies. I shall assist you in any way I can. You may come to me tomorrow morning at ten."

Lord Davies rose and bowed low. To his credit, none of his horror at the desecration of his boot or the early hour Miss Pymbroke set for his call showed on his face as he made his way out of the house.

Feeling a warm glow at being needed, Verity rose and straightened her skirt. On her way out of the room, she glanced over to where Empress, bored already with her new toy, flicked the tassel carelessly under a chair.

As she climbed the stairs she reflected on the turn of events with Lord Davies. Her feeling that there was good in everyone was often confirmed in the unlikeliest ways. Who would have imagined Lord Davies's visit?

It almost gave her hope where the Marquess of Carrisworth was concerned.

Almost.

Upon entering Lord and Lady Lexham's townhouse in Park Lane, Verity drew in an awed breath at her grand surroundings. About thirty guests were assembled in the large gold drawing room, which blazed with candlelight and a rich display of gleaming wood, shining satins, and heavy velvets. Several ornate paintings had been mounted *on top* of the wall's tapestries, a move designed to serve as further proof of the host's great wealth. A group of musicians had been engaged for the evening and were sedately playing Mozart.

Accompanied by Louisa and the Ladies Iris and Hyacinth, Verity felt grateful that Beecham had once again taken charge of her appearance. She was wearing a white silk gown with a gold braid trim, which repeated at the round neck, the high waist, and the hem. The gown's tiny sleeves were puffed, and long white gloves covered her arms. White silk roses with seed pearls forming their centers had been carefully placed in her hair.

At her side, Louisa did not bother to conceal her boredom and promptly went off in search of a glass of wine.

Lady Hyacinth, in her usual bundle of shawls, walked beside Verity as they made their way through the room. She gently squeezed Verity's arm and confided, "Do not be intimidated, dear child. I happen to know Lady Lexham periodically hires a certain French hairdresser to shave off a truly horrendous mustache that grows above her upper lip. Why she does not ask him to take care of her chin, I cannot conceive," she mused.

"Eudora," Lady Iris was saying as Lady Lexham approached them. "Let me present Miss Verity Pymbroke. She is staying with Hyacinth and me for the Season."

Verity curtsyed low to the formidable lady clad in a purple taffeta dress and matching turban. Upon rising, she found herself being coldly scrutinized. She tried hard not to return the stare when her gaze rested on the ugly white hairs sprouting from the lady's chin.

"Pretty gel," Lady Lexham allowed haughtily when she'd finished her inspection. "I'll make her known to my youngest son, Lord Peter."

Lady Lexham signaled to a nervous-looking young man of about twenty-five years, who, in the manner of one long used to doing his mother's bidding, immediately crossed to her side and bowed over Verity's hand. She thought him not unattractive with his blond hair done in the Windswept and his clear blue eyes, which observed her shyly.

The older people melted away, leaving Verity and Lord Peter standing alone. "Are you, um, making your come-out this Season, Miss Pymbroke?" Lord Peter ventured politely.

"Well, not exactly. I mean, this is my first year of going about in Society," Verity answered, unsure of how much to tell him. But she needn't have worried as the young peer's attention was not on her reply.

"I say, who was that . . . um, deucedly pretty lady who arrived in your party? She is sitting, um, across the room."

Verity looked over to where Louisa sat petulantly sipping from a glass of champagne. Her gown of azure tissue floated around her. "My sister, Mrs. Barrington. Shall I make her known to you?"

"Oh, yes, um, please," Lord Peter said breathily.

Louisa, whose tastes did not generally run to younger sons, nevertheless was bored enough to be pleased by Lord Peter's flattering attentions.

Verity turned away, telling herself she was glad Lord Peter had shown an interest in her sister. He was surely better for her than Sir Ramsey.

However, she could barely cloak her dismay when moments later Mr. Cecil Sedgewick entered the room with Lady Foxworth and a simpering Lady Althea.

"Lady Lexham appears to be remiss in the selection of her guests," a feminine voice declared at Verity's side. "Surely there are more ladies here tonight than gentlemen, which is really too bad."

Verity turned to find a beautiful lady in burgundy silk smiling at her. Blue eyes sparkled from a heart-shaped face of a flawless complexion. Masses of heavy, honey-blonde hair were pinned into a becoming style that threatened to fall down the lady's back any moment.

"It was rather shabby of Lady Lexham," Verity replied, liking the lady at once and unable to repress a smile. "I am Miss Verity Pymbroke."

"And I am Cynthia, Countess of Northbridge. I came

here with my husband, but the wretch has wandered away to look for a friend of ours who was to meet us but is late. Are you an acquaintance of Lady Lexham? I have not seen you before but confess I have been out of Town much of late and am not *au courant* with Society."

"I met Lady Lexham this evening and am here with the two older ladies I live with, Lady Iris and Lady Hyacinth."

Lady Northbridge nodded. "I know the dears, of course." Lowering her voice to a conspiratorial whisper, the countess asked, "Does Lady Hyacinth still tell those bouncers about her, er, past gentleman callers?"

Verity chuckled. "Yes, indeed she does, my lady."

"Please, call me Cynthia. I hope we can be friends."

Verity hoped so too. She had never had a female friend who was close to her in age. And the countess appeared kind and positively radiated happiness.

Their burgeoning friendship was put to the test a few moments later, however, when Cynthia's husband returned with the missing guest. Verity was barely able to perform her part in the introductions that followed. Her heart was thudding painfully, and she felt sure a telltale blush colored her cheeks when she looked up into a pair of familiar, amused green eyes.

In a lazy voice, the marquess said, "But, Cynthia, Miss Pymbroke and I already know each other, for she is my own sweet landlady." He bowed low before grasping Verity's gloved hand and bestowing a kiss upon it.

Lest he begin caressing it in his usual manner, Verity tugged her hand away.

Demands for an explanation of how the marquess came to be leasing a house from Miss Pymbroke resulted in Lord Carrisworth telling a sugarcoated version of the facts. During this discourse, he never once took his teasing gaze from her face.

Missing the speculative gleam in Cynthia's eyes, Verity used the time to try to bring her emotions under control. She was surprised to see the marquess at such a genteel entertainment and in the company of Lord and Lady Northbridge, a respectable married couple obviously very much in love.

In spite of herself, her gaze moved to the marquess's firm mouth and memories of the previous evening flooded back.

At that moment, Lady Lexham called her guests to the massive dining room. She had a cross look on her face, the result of her son's flirtation with a widow and the unwelcome presence at her dinner of a known rake. In addition, her distraught butler had whispered some ridiculous tale of the cook, Mrs. Witherspoon, trying to take liberties with him.

Lord Carrisworth offered Verity his arm, and since she could not refuse without seeming churlish, she accepted it. The dining room was every bit as ornate as the gold drawing room. The long table shone with polished silver. Three large silver epergnes brimming with hothouse fruits graced the table at carefully placed intervals.

Verity hoped she might seat herself as far away as possible from the marquess, but these hopes were quickly dashed when she realized a liveried footman was holding out a chair for her and Lord Carrisworth immediately chose the one next to it.

Lady Iris and Lady Hyacinth were seated across from her with an older gentleman, introduced as Lord Killigrew, between them. Lord Killigrew was obviously puffed up with his own importance, and his heavy jowls gave him the appearance of a surly old bulldog.

Mr. Cecil Sedgewick sat on Verity's other side, much to her delight. But, before she could begin a conversation with the cleric, who was helping Lady Althea to a seat on his other side, Lord Carrisworth addressed her. "Miss Pymbroke, you are not going to make a fuss over last night, are you?"

Verity raised her chin, but kept her voice low. "I displayed a criminal lack of sense by getting into a closed carriage with you, my lord. I suppose, knowing what you are, I can hardly blame you for taking advantage of me."

Lord Carrisworth had been watching her with half-closed eyes. At these last words, however, his lids snapped open. He suddenly wished to shock her into betraying her feelings. Into telling him she had been plagued with memories of their kiss all day, just as he had been. "From your passionate response I could only conclude you welcomed my embrace."

Verity seethed with anger and humiliation. Impossible man! How dare he remind her of her behavior? "You are mistaken, my lord," she lied. "Ladies do not have the same lusts and passions as men do."

The marquess dropped his lids back down over his eyes to conceal his irritation. Little baggage, denying the truth in that scornful way. He had a mind to prove to her right then and there how her lips would respond under his.

Fortunately for the inflamed pair, a footman appeared at Verity's elbow, carrying a silver tureen in the shape of a large clam shell. The shell stood above three silver seahorses rising from a triangular base worked in imitation of waves. The footman raised the cover, its handle shaped like a merman, to reveal the turtle soup, which looked unremarkable despite the fact Molly had laced it with Love's Helping Hand.

Verity wrinkled her nose. When she was a little girl, her mother employed a cook who liked to display the skulls of turtles she had used for turtle soup on the walls of the kitchen. Exploring the kitchens at the tender age of four, Verity had been sufficiently frightened by the skulls to conceive a permanent dislike of turtle soup. Many years later when the cook had been pensioned off, Verity had immediately given the order for the skulls to be taken down.

Now, she shook her head at the waiting footman who then offered the soup to Lord Carrisworth. The marquess also denied him, wishing to continue his conversation with the infuriating Miss Pymbroke unencumbered by food.

But in this he was thwarted as Verity turned away to speak to Mr. Sedgewick. Draining his wineglass in frustration, the marquess decided he would not help Miss Pymbroke win the cleric's affection after all.

Verity gave Mr. Sedgewick a friendly smile. "I am glad of this opportunity to speak to you. I have not seen you of late and miss our conversations."

Cecil Sedgewick's owl-like eyes peered at her above his glasses. "I understand you dropped your work with the actresses," he replied with a hint of accusation.

"Well, yes. My sister has returned from Spain—"

Mr. Sedgewick interrupted her, saying, "Yes, I imagined your efforts would be taken up with her."

Verity paused. For a moment it had almost seemed as if Mr. Sedgewick were sneering at Louisa. But no, he would never be unkind. She tried for a change in subject. "You may be interested to know Lord Davies came to me only this morning asking for instruction. I was very flattered that he thought of me. Is it not wonderful when a man can admit his character can be improved?"

Mr. Sedgewick's spoon clattered into his bowl of soup. Shaking his balding head, he said, "Worse and worse. First the Marquess of Carrisworth, now Lord Davies. Miss Pymbroke, you poor misguided female, how does a lady I had always thought of as having a superior sense of the proprieties become involved with such low fellows?"

Before Verity had a chance to answer this insulting question, Mr. Sedgewick continued. "I am most disappointed in you, Miss Pymbroke. Rumor has it you have gone so far as to appear at a masked ball. Tsk! It is indeed a shame."

With these words of condemnation, he turned firmly away to Lady Althea.

Verity sat through the rest of the courses, plagued with doubts. Toying with her food, she wondered at the severity of Mr. Sedgewick's displeasure. He had not even given her a chance to explain.

Had he formed a *tendre* for the long-nosed Lady Althea? Unbidden, the marquess's words came back to her. *Your Mr. Sedgewick is toadying quite dreadfully to Lady Althea and her mother in the hopes of obtaining a living.* Naturally, Verity thought bitterly, if this were true it would not do for Mr. Sedgewick to be seen continuing a friendship with another lady. Perhaps he simply wished to cut their connection.

She glanced at Lord Carrisworth. He was speaking to Louisa, seated on his other side. Verity's brows came together abruptly. Was not Louisa leaning awfully close to the marquess?

In fact, as Verity glanced around the table, it suddenly seemed as if several couples were brushing hands or exchanging speaking looks. Voices grew louder and giddy laughter filled the room. How singular.

Eventually the meal ended and, as one, the gentlemen decided to forgo their port. Everyone retired to the gold drawing room, where due to a miracle wrought by a horde of servants, the furniture had been removed so there might be dancing.

Louisa entered the room, clinging to Lord Peter's arm. He shouted to the musicians, "A waltz!" Immediately, the floor was filled with swaying couples. Lord Peter grabbed Louisa in what he thought was a masterful way and led her onto the floor. Since he secretly thought of himself as a blond Lord Byron, he stared morosely down at Louisa while they danced.

Verity's mouth dropped open as she watched Louisa gazing up at the young man seductively.

Suddenly, Cynthia was at Verity's side with her husband. "My dear Verity, Charles and I must leave. I shall call on you."

"I should like that, Cynthia," Verity replied.

"Let us go *now*, Excellent," Lord Northbridge commanded and led his unprotesting wife quickly out of the room.

Lady Althea was dancing with Mr. Sedgewick. Every moment or so, she let out a scream of laughter that filled the room with its intensity. Verity was shocked down to her soul to see Mr. Sedgewick holding Lady Althea much more closely than was proper.

Verity was not the only one noticing the change in the guests. Lord Carrisworth leaned against the fireplace, taking in the scene with an amused expression on his handsome face. One would almost think some of Lady Iris's potion had been served the assembly, he thought.

A look of alarm crossed his features. Then, he relaxed. No, he distinctly remembered ordering Millweed to dispose of the stuff. In any case, it would not do for the innocent Miss Pymbroke to remain in this company. He determined to find Lady Iris.

In an unprecedented move, Lady Hyacinth had thrown off her shawls and was dancing with Lord Killigrew, who had lost his sour bulldog expression and was, instead, gazing at Lady Hyacinth like a young puppy.

Verity pressed her fingers to her temples and decided everyone had gone mad.

In a strange twist of circumstance, Lady Iris had not partaken of the turtle soup. She came up to Verity, saying loudly, "Hyacinth never could leave anything in breeches alone. And just look at your sister. Once a slut, always a slut."

Verity looked in the direction Lady Iris indicated and gasped. Louisa and Lord Peter had stolen behind a potted plant, not quite out of view, and were locked in each other's arms.

Lady Iris snorted and banged her cane on the floor. "Dash my wig! This affair is turning into a disgrace. I'm going to fetch our cloaks and get us out of here. Oh, good. Carrisworth, stand guard over Verity until I return. Great bunch of people here acting crazy. I don't know what's gotten into 'em."

Verity fought to control her swirling emotions. Her eyes had taken on the blank look of one in shock. The marquess gently led her out into the empty hall. "If you concentrate, Miss Pymbroke, you can hear the music out here." He bowed formally and whispered, "May I have this dance?"

Numbly, Verity stepped toward him, then stopped, glancing nervously around her. Her voice weak, she said, "My lord, the rules of proper behavior state a lady would never dance with a partner alone in a deserted hall."

Paying no attention to this protest, Lord Carrisworth

placed one arm about her waist and grasped her gloved hand in his. The effect of being so close to him caused a delicious shudder of heat to race through her veins and make her frozen blood thaw.

A hot ache grew in her throat.

The marquess's hand tightened on the small of her back. They stared at each other, both suddenly having difficulty breathing.

From the drawing room, Lady Lexham's voice rang out. "Peter! Take your hands off that trollop!"

Verity blinked her eyes rapidly and broke away from his arms. "My lord, my sister . . . I must take her away."

Damn! Always her sister or Cecil Sedgewick or her bloody principles!

"Yes, the discreet Mrs. Barrington," he ground out. "Now there is an example of your earlier assertions. What was it again? Ah yes, ladies do not have the same lusts and passions as men." Turning on his heel, he strode back into the drawing room.

Verity watched him go, her eyes wide, her heart pounding furiously in her chest. "I believe they do after all," she whispered with dawning realization to the uncaring balustrade.

Chapter Seven

Clad in a lawn nightdress with ribbons at the beruffled neck, Verity sat in bed drinking her morning chocolate.

Hearing the sounds of paws scratching on the bedside table, she turned her head and saw Empress standing on her hind legs. The cat stretched a dainty paw out in an effort to capture the ribbon tied on the miniature Verity had found in her father's room.

"Empress! No!" Placing the breakfast tray aside, Verity reached over and picked up the miniature.

The silver-colored cat leaped across the table, upending a thankfully unlit candle, and onto the bed. She jumped across Verity's lap to chase the dangling ribbon. The dishes on the breakfast tray rattled noisily, threatening to spill across the olive green coverlet.

"You may not have it," Verity said and chuckled. She quickly opened the drawer of the table and popped the miniature inside, slamming the compartment shut in front of the frustrated cat's face. There followed a five-minute session of patting, stroking, and complimenting before she could restore Empress's equanimity.

During this time, Verity pondered over the lady of the miniature, their father's mistress. Louisa had said she was Mary Jennings, the actress. Had her father loved the woman? Or had he simply been running away from the responsibilities of his family?

Verity leaned back against her pillows and closed her eyes, still stroking Empress. For some inexplicable reason her thoughts veered sharply to the marquess. Had it been kindness that motivated him to try to shield her from the scandalous goings-on in the Lexhams' drawing room by taking her in his arms for that waltz in the hall?

Despite all her resolutions to keep her distance from him, she seemed destined to cross his path. And what was worse, she was not as adverse to his company as her sensible side felt she ought to be.

Was it possible he cared about her? His actions at the Lexhams, as well as that dreadful masked ball, seemed to indicate he did.

But of course, a little voice sneered in her brain, a rake knew just how to manage his victim. After the masked ball, while in his carriage, had he not extracted a price for his services in the form of that never-to-be-forgotten kiss?

"I've pressed the white-striped muslin gown, miss," Betty said, entering the room. "Are you ready to dress for Lord Davies's visit?"

Opening her eyes, Verity threw off the bedcover and said, "Yes, thank you, Betty. I had almost forgotten Lord Davies will be here at ten."

The maid removed the breakfast tray while her mistress washed and then helped her dress. "You'll need to wear the pink garters today, miss. The red silk ones need mending."

"Very well," Verity said. Her mind was already on what she would discuss with Lord Davies. She hoped he would be receptive to her thoughts on how Society could help fallen women.

Finished dressing, Verity walked out of the room to go downstairs. Betty gathered her mistress's clothing for laundering. She didn't notice when one red silk garter slid to the floor.

Empress, ever alert, sprang from the bed where she'd been watching the proceedings and pounced on the frilly garter. Holding it in her mouth by one of its ribbons, the cat paraded from the room.

The Marquess of Carrisworth sat alone on a marble bench in Verity's garden reading the *Times*. He had just come in from his now customary early morning ride in the Park, and after changing clothes had found himself drawn back to the sunny outdoors. Amazing, he thought, how keeping a clear head the night before resulted in feeling fit in the morning.

"My lord," an elderly voice croaked from the doorway, "I thought I understood it to be one of Miss Pymbroke's rules that you not use her back garden."

His lordship lowered the newspaper and turned to scowl at Mr. Wetherall. "Miss Pymbroke has too many rules. Besides, what harm can there be in sitting out among these beautiful roses?"

The old valet's left eye twitched, and he came outside to stand over the marquess like a stern father. "The flowers are pretty. They've been raised well. Just like the young lady. Tempting she is, like being out here when you're not supposed to."

Lord Carrisworth's expression grew chilly. "I always do just as I please, and you know it."

"Yes, my lord," Mr. Wetherall agreed. "Anyhow, what I hear from the servants about Miss Pymbroke tells me she's a right 'un, good-hearted, too. Cared for her Mama until the end and never complained about not attending balls and parties and such."

The marquess took his gaze from the valet's piercing eyes and examined a rose close to the bench where he was seated. Putting the newspaper aside, he reached out, pulled the flower to him, and drew in its potent fragrance. He suddenly recalled Miss Pymbroke wore a light rose-scented perfume. "What is your point, man? You are wasting your breath if you think to tell me the lady is not to be toyed with. I already know it."

Mr. Wetherall's wrinkled face was expressionless. "Of course, my lord. Miss Pymbroke is, as you say, the type you would marry."

"I never said that, you old devil!" Lord Carrisworth responded in a fit of acute aggravation. "I shall never marry." But he spoke to the valet's retreating back.

"By God, was ever a man so plagued? My own servant has turned matchmaker." The marquess jerked the flower, pulling it from its stem. "Damme," he said through gritted teeth. A particularly large thorn had objected to his treatment of the blossom, resulting in a line of blood across Lord Carrisworth's palm.

Using his handkerchief to clean his hand, he was reminded of the day he first met the angelic Miss Pymbroke and her adorably outraged reaction when he had acted as if he would kiss her thorn-pricked finger. How prim and proper she had been. Such a contrast to the way she had behaved in his carriage. His lordship groaned in frustration at the memory.

As if to underline Verity's passionate side, Empress appeared balancing on the wall of the garden, the red silk garter clamped in her jaws. Spying the marquess, she made a magnificent jump down to the ground and padded gracefully over to where he sat, dragging the garter behind her. Reaching him, she stood on her delicate hind legs and deposited the red silk garter in his lap.

"Good God, first a matchmaking servant and now a matchmaking cat." Lord Carrisworth rolled his eyes. "I assume this belongs to Mrs. Barrington?"

Empress's whiskers turned down. She removed her front paws from where they had been resting on his lordship's buff pantaloons. Standing on the ground, she glared at him and, as if in extreme distaste, she shook her right front paw.

The marquess observed these actions and interpreted them as a negative. "You mean to tell me this belongs to Miss Pymbroke?"

"Miaow," Empress promptly answered, her fluffy tail swaying sinuously.

"Yes, now that I think on it, as unlikely as it might at first seem, I believe you."

Hastily, the marquess rose to his feet and balled up the piece of silk, thrusting it into his pocket. Irrationally, he felt it would scorch his hand if he continued holding it. Intent on returning the lacy scrap to its owner, he strode through the glass doors, across the cheerful yellow morning room, into the hall, and out the front door. Just in time to see a smiling Miss Pymbroke being driven away by Lord Davies in his high-perch phaeton in the direction of the Park.

Lord Carrisworth retreated into the house and slammed the front door, startling the butler. "Have my carriage brought round, Digby," he barked out.

The marquess paced the black-and-white tiled hallway, slapping his gloves against his thigh. He would drive after them and discover what Miss Pymbroke was about, allowing herself to be escorted by the dandified baron. She was such an innocent. Evidently she had not learned her lesson regarding Lord Davies that day at the theater. How the man could even see Verity over his ridiculously high shirt points was beyond imagination, he reflected in disgust.

A few minutes passed while he waited for his vehicle, during which time his temper gradually cooled. Reason asked him what he was doing storming after the chit like a jealous lover. Her activities were nothing to do with him. He had no right. He had nothing to offer her.

Well, that wasn't precisely true. He had something he was aching to offer her. But it wasn't marriage, the only proposition he could respectably make.

"Bloody hell," he muttered. Seeing his tiger outside with the carriage at last, he made up his mind. "White's," he shouted, climbing into the vehicle.

An afternoon of drinking and gaming at his club was what he needed. Imagine, a man of the town like himself growing maudlin over a proper young miss. Ridiculous!

Watching from the landing above, Mr. Wetherall thought he'd never seen his normally languid lordship so agitated. If that don't beat the Dutch! He rubbed his wrinkled old hands together gleefully, cackling with laughter as he turned to make his way down the corridor.

Plump in the pocket after the sale of Love's Helping Hand, Lady Iris took Verity and Lady Hyacinth on a rare shopping expedition later that day.

Lady Hyacinth was in high alt because of her restored credit at Mr. Millweed's shop and couldn't wait to try a new potion made by a lady who called herself Auntie Payne.

Over Verity's protests, Lady Iris purchased a length of gold-colored silk for her young friend. "I shan't hear another word, gel. The shade will be flattering on you, and you need a new evening gown," Lady Iris proclaimed after concluding arrangements with the dressmaker. Secretly she viewed the stunning creation the modiste had promised as the very thing required to permanently fix Lord Carrisworth's interest in the girl.

"But, my lady, Beecham has done wonders working over Louisa's gowns. I shall do very well with what I have," Verity persisted while being led out of the shop.

"That's all well and good. But you deserve a gown made just for you. Not any more of your sister's castoffs that have probably had some man's hands run all over them—and under them," Lady Iris concluded with a derisive snort.

"I am not one to correct my elders, Lady Iris, but I must ask you to refrain from speaking of my sister in that manner." A footman helped the three ladies into their carriage. Seating herself next to Lady Hyacinth in the coach, Verity stiffened her spine.

In the face of what promised to be an extended discussion, Lady Hyacinth held up her plump hands in a pleading gesture. "Iris, you promised we might go to Gunter's for an ice. You know I cannot last more than two hours without taking sustenance else I shall have a spasm." Raising a hand to her brow, she said feebly, "Indeed, I grow weaker every moment."

Lady Iris eyed her sister sourly but gave the order to the coachman for Berkeley Square. Gunter's was the only place in Mayfair where ladies could go unescorted to take tea or enjoy some of the celebrated ices and sorbets said to be prepared from a secret recipe.

After settling themselves at a table in Gunter's, they placed their orders for ices. Verity could barely enjoy the treat when it was placed in front of her because, sitting across from her, Lady Iris was once again speaking derisively of Louisa.

"The woman is no better than she should be. I know she's your sister"—Lady Iris paused to glower at Lady Hyacinth who had rapidly finished her ice and was ordering another—"but one can't choose one's relatives, more's the pity. Louisa is liable to damage your reputation while you try in vain to save hers."

Verity's gaze was on her plate. "You make it sound as if there is no good in Louisa."

"I'm certain she excels at some things," Lady Iris replied, her gruff voice sarcastic. Then her tone softened. "What I'm saying is we all have choices in life, gel. Your sister has made hers, and you cannot allow yourself to suffer needlessly from them. We can only hope Louisa will marry before she puts herself completely beyond the pale."

"I can help her, if she will only listen to me," Verity insisted, but knowing in her mind that what Lady Iris said was the truth. It was her heart that refused to give up on Louisa.

Lady Iris shook her bewigged head sadly. "Why not concentrate on your own future? You know you are welcome to remain with Hyacinth and me after the Season and continue to lease out your townhouse, but you should have a husband."

A vision of the Marquess of Carrisworth's handsome face materialized in Verity's mind, and she dropped her spoon on her plate with a clink. Despite her growing attraction to him, he was anything but a suitable candidate for her husband. Besides which, he wouldn't want a wife. Why then could she not seem to stop thinking of him?

Oblivious to the turn her young friend's thoughts had

taken, Lady Iris said, "I know you mean well, but one cannot change other people, Verity, no matter how badly one wants to."

The waiter arrived at the table with yet another strawberry ice for Lady Hyacinth.

"Only consider my dolt of a sister," Lady Iris continued wrathfully. "I've warned her time out of number that too many sweets are bad for her health. Ye gods, is that your third, Hyacinth? Give me that plate!"

Lady Iris reached across the table and grasped the dish of strawberry ice. Lady Hyacinth hung on for dear life. "No! Take your hands off it, Iris!"

The two ladies gripped the plate, each trying to wrest it from the other's grasp. Suddenly, with a burst of strength, Lady Hyacinth succeeded in pulling it from Lady Iris. But the force catapulted the contents of the dish up and across the older lady's shoulder.

Twisting round in her chair, Lady Hyacinth saw with chagrin that her ice had splashed across the back of another customer's superbly tailored coat. The offended gentleman rose and turned to face his assailant.

To her horror, Lady Hyacinth recognized the famous dandy and social leader, Beau Brummell.

There was sudden, absolute silence in the shop as everyone stared. Feeling as if she had been plunged into the worst of nightmares, Lady Hyacinth gave a little cry and slumped over her place at the table in a swoon.

Alarmed, Verity spared not a glimpse at Mr. Brummell. Instead, she reached for her napkin and wetted it with water from her glass. She patted the dampened cloth about Lady Hyacinth's temples and the back of her neck. "My lady, please, you must wake up."

"She's probably pretending," Lady Iris accused. "Get up, Hyacinth, you buffleheaded gudgeon."

Meanwhile, waiters came running up offering towels to their powerful guest, but Brummell froze them with a glance. The friend accompanying him, "Poodle" Byng, picked up a napkin and quickly wiped the sticky mess from the Beau's ruined coat.

Slowly, Lady Hyacinth came round, moaning and clutching the edge of the table. "My vinaigrette . . ." she uttered weakly.

Verity hastened to retrieve the container from her ladyship's reticule and waved it under the older lady's nose.

"Oh, Hyacinth, you ninny," Lady Iris said, and was assailed by a fit of laughter so convulsive, the crescent-shaped patch she wore by her mouth loosened and fell into her own ice, causing her to laugh even harder.

Everyone in Mayfair knew one another so Brummell realized with whom he was dealing. He bowed and said, "Good afternoon, Lady Iris. Lady Hyacinth, I should have been pleased to join you for an ice had your invitation been less imaginative."

Lady Hyacinth's expression cleared and she giggled like a schoolgirl. "Oh, my dear Mr. Brummell, you are everything kind. And after I ruined your handsome coat. It does show the strength and width of your shoulders particularly well. How will you ever forgive me?"

"What a fustian," Lady Iris mumbled crossly.

The Beau, completely disarmed by Lady Hyacinth's flattery, took one of her hands and raised it to his lips. "A beautiful lady must always be forgiven, else she might remove herself from the presence of admiring eyes." His gaze moved to Verity and he raised an inquiring brow.

Lady Iris performed the introductions since Lady Hyacinth was busy fluttering her eyelashes at Mr. Brummell. He said, "Ah, yes, Miss Pymbroke, I have heard you are leasing your townhouse to Carrisworth. Rather like the lamb allowing the wolf through the front door, is it not?"

Poodle, Brummell's table companion, raised an eyebrow. "I say, that's not quite fair, is it? The word in the clubs is that Carrisworth has given his mistresses their *congé.*"

The Beau turned a haughty look on his friend. "Have you been spending too much time in the company of your dog? Ladies are present. Your conversation is not fit for their ears."

Poodle inclined his head. "So terribly sorry, ladies. Forgot myself."

Verity's heart beat hard. The marquess had ended his relationship with the French girls! What could have caused this change of heart? She knew her cheeks were pink, but managed to meet the Beau's gaze without flinching. "I am happy to meet you, sir."

Brummell's eyes twinkled. "I hope I may have the honor of a dance at the Tremaines' ball tomorrow night."

After receiving a nod from Lady Iris indicating they would be attending, Verity responded, "I should like it above all things."

Turning to Lady Hyacinth he said, "While the loss of my coat grieves me excessively, you must not blame yourself. I had quite decided the color will be out of fashion tomorrow."

He gave the ladies an elegant bow, picked up his walking stick, and strolled out of Gunter's with his friend in tow.

Lady Hyacinth sang the praises of Mr. Brummell the entire way home in the coach. "Such a nice young man, not at all high in the instep. Did you mark the speaking way he looked at me, Iris?"

"Depend upon it, he's top over heels in love with you, Hyacinth," Lady Iris said dryly.

Lady Hyacinth chose to ignore her sister's mockery. Patting her red curls she said, "He is very close with the Prince Regent, Iris, and as I've tried to explain to you before, our Regent prefers plump, slightly older ladies. It stands to reason Mr. Brummell's tastes would run parallel to our dear Prinny's."

Verity turned her head to hide a smile.

"Tarnation!" Lady Iris expostulated, "Of course the Regent would want a larger lady. In bed, a smaller one might be crushed to death under his massive weight. Think of the scandal."

Lady Hyacinth drew her shawls around her tightly. "You have always been jealous of me, Iris."

"Home at last," Verity announced trying to divert the sisters' attention before the situation escalated to one of their famous quarrels.

"There is Lord Carrisworth," Lady Hyacinth declared, stepping down from the carriage. Her welcoming smile died on her lips. "Oh dear, his lordship has brought a lady friend home. He seems a bit unsteady on his feet."

Verity alighted from the vehicle and halted on the sidewalk. Her gaze flew to where the marquess, who looked like the very devil, was mounting the steps of *her* townhouse with Roxanna clinging to his arm. The actress threw Verity a smug look over her shoulder, then disappeared inside with Lord Carrisworth, who had obviously drunk enough to make a cat speak.

Lady Iris cursed under her breath. Then she caught sight of the unmistakably hurt look on Verity's face. Ah, the darling girl was not indifferent to him. Well, she would simply have to put Verity in the way of understanding it was to be expected that Carrisworth wouldn't give up his vulgar flirts entirely.

Verity's lips compressed. After she'd asked him specifically not to, here he was bringing one of his doxies home—to her house. Detestable man, she thought, feeling a tightening in her throat and a constriction in her chest.

Holding herself in strict control, she walked up the steps behind Lady Iris and Lady Hyacinth and through the door Bingwood opened. Calmly excusing herself, she climbed the stairs and found her way to her bedchamber, quietly closing the door behind her.

Then she advanced but a few steps into the room and threw her reticule with unnecessary force onto the bed.

"Damn the ground you swagger upon, my Lord Carrisworth," murmured the proper Miss Pymbroke, who had given many a lecture to others on not using profanity.

"Mrs. Barrington has gone off again, miss."

Sitting in the drawing room with Lady Iris and Lady Hyacinth, Verity looked at the maid in surprise. "What? Louisa is to go with us to Lady Graham's musicale."

"Well, she's left the house and that's a fact," Betty advised. "Mr. Bingwood himself opened the door to Sir Ramsey a few minutes ago. And while you know the butler ain't one for gossip, I was coming down the stairs with Mrs. Barrington's shawl when he says, 'You are too late, Betty, madam has left with Sir Ramsey for the opening night at Vauxhall.'"

"How romantic," Lady Hyacinth cried. "Why I remember many magical nights at Vauxhall listening to the music, watching the fireworks, and especially strolling down the Lover's Walk with one of my handsome gallants. Oh, how the gentlemen do misbehave themselves along the darkened walkways!"

Verity listened with growing concern. Surely it was not wise for Louisa to attend the pleasure gardens alone with Sir Ramsey. "I must go and find her. Betty, run upstairs for my cloak."

Lady Hyacinth's face had taken on a dreamy expression. "I remember one evening in particular when dear Lord Anthony plucked one of the plumes from my headdress and ran it up and down—"

"Just like Cleopatra," Lady Iris interrupted pettishly. "Verity, we are engaged to the Grahams. Leave Louisa to her fate."

"Indeed, my lady, I cannot. I shall take Betty along with me—"

"Hmph. After she deserted you at that masked ball? Fat lot of protection she would be. Besides, I refuse to let your selfish sister ruin our evening."

Lady Hyacinth drew all five feet two inches of herself up straight. She stared at Lady Iris while addressing Verity. "Never mind, dear child, *I* shall accompany you. I have a mind to see Vauxhall again."

Lady Iris threw up her hands in defeat. "A pox on all sisters! Go then, but I'll not be a party to such foolishness." So saying, her ladyship retrieved her cane and stomped away.

The minute Lady Iris left the room, Lady Hyacinth seemed to deflate. "Oh dear. Perhaps it would be better if we had a gentleman to escort us. I'll send a footman next door and ask the marquess—"

"No!" Verity denied her. "Not him. I shall ask . . ." Verity thought fleetingly of Cecil Sedgewick. But he had not called after Lady Lexham's turtle dinner, and she shuddered remembering the censure in his conversation with her. She had only one other choice. "Lord Davies."

Verity hurried along the Grand Walk at Vauxhall desperately searching for her sister. The black gauze mantle, which she wore over a white muslin dress with a spencer bodice of pale blue, flew out behind her.

By the time Lord Davies had been summoned and had conveyed them to the famous pleasure gardens, she had worked herself up into a frenzy of agitation. Certain Louisa needed her as never before, she rushed headlong to the Grand Cross Walk, which ran through the center of the grounds, unaware of her companions' distress.

Lord Davies was heartily sick of the game. "My dear Miss Pymbroke, surely any sister of yours must be above reproach. Why, we are putting Lady Hyacinth's health at risk by jaunting about in this manner." Lord Davies congratulated himself on this thoughtful statement. In truth, he was obsessed with a fear his brand-new Hessian boots—which he'd picked up from Hoby's only that day, being forced to fork over the blunt for a new pair after that contemptible cat had ruined his others—would be scraped during their mad dash.

"Indeed, dear child," Lady Hyacinth gasped, trying to catch her breath. "I cannot go on. Why I expect at any moment to turn my ankle running about on this frightful gravel—"

"There she is!" Verity exclaimed triumphantly. Leaving behind an open-mouthed Lady Hyacinth and a grim-faced Lord Davies, she ran ahead to where Louisa and Sir Ramsey were disappearing down the walkway.

"Oh dear," moaned Lady Hyacinth to Lord Davies, who had raised his quizzing glass and was trying to discreetly inspect his boots for damage in the dim light. "What are we to do?"

At that moment Lord Killigrew appeared, his heavy jowls trembling as he walked down the path. "Your servant, Lady Hyacinth," he said and bowed. "How charming to meet you again so soon after Lady Lexham's turtle dinner."

Something had been rejuvenated in the older man, that something being in his breeches, after his experience with Love's Helping Hand. He had come to the gardens seeking female company and was not adverse to assisting Lord Davies in taking care of Lady Hyacinth in her hour of need.

That lady quickly apprised the gentleman of their situation. Lord Killigrew appeared all concern. "Pray allow me to escort you to a supper box, Lady Hyacinth. I am persuaded you would be more comfortable with a bite to eat while Lord Davies follows Miss Pymbroke."

Since nothing could be more to her ladyship's liking, Lady Hyacinth accepted Lord Killigrew's arm with a smile and the two moved away.

Lord Davies was left alone to brood in sulky silence. Lounging against a tree, he decided to wait where he was. He would not risk his boots by dragging them through the shrubbery. Eventually, the stupid girl would have to come back this way.

Meanwhile, Verity looked frantically for her sister. She dared not call out her name and thus reveal her identity. Following the couple who were ahead of her, Verity realized the walkway they were now on was quite narrow and dark. Quickening her steps, she experienced a shiver of fear and bit her lip to keep it from trembling. All at once she stumbled upon Louisa who was returning a passionate kiss from Sir Ramsey.

"Louisa, thank goodness I have found you!"

Swiftly, the couple broke apart. Sir Ramsey's face held an amused expression. Louisa was breathless with rage. Rancor sharpened her voice. "Randy, my love, I wish to speak privately with my sister. Wait for me at our box."

Sir Ramsey shrugged his shoulders and bowed, leaving the two women alone.

In the face of Louisa's fury, Verity felt a chill run down her spine. Nonetheless, she forced herself to say the words uppermost in her thoughts. "My dear sister, please come home with me. Surely you see Sir Ramsey is not fit company. A gentleman never k-kisses a l-lady," she stammered, a sudden vision of Lord Carrisworth kissing her in his carriage forming in her mind, "unless they are betrothed and you have not indicated—"

"I shall kiss whom I please, where I please!" Louisa screeched. "How dare you follow me here, you interfering, moralizing, *silly* little fool," she spat out contemptuously.

Verity drew in her breath sharply. "Louisa, I thought we loved each other. Could I have been mistaken?"

"Love?" the widow questioned derisively. "There is no such thing. Only lust."

"But, your husband, Philip, you loved him," Verity whispered, her brown eyes enormous in her face.

Louisa laughed briefly. "Of course not, though I didn't know it at the time. I simply wanted him in my bed. But I am no longer a green-head. When I marry, it will be for wealth and position, and I shall seek my pleasures elsewhere. Oh, stop gaping at me like a stuck pig."

"Louisa, you must not say such things," Verity said faintly.

The widow took a menacing step toward her. "And

you, my meddling Mouse, will keep out of my affairs from this second forward. Do I make myself clear?"

Verity felt sick. She realized that what Lady Iris had been telling her all along about Louisa was true. "I understand," she replied sadly.

Louisa flashed her a look of disdain. "A martyr to the bitter end."

At the look on her sister's face, Verity took a step backward and stumbled. Her arms flailed out at her sides, and she landed in the gravel on her posterior.

At that moment, the nearby sounds of drunken male laughter floated on the air. Louisa's stormy gray eyes narrowed. In a second they would be upon them. Without another look toward her sister's plight, Louisa turned and ran away down the path, just as three very drunk young men, looking for a girl to drag off into the shrubbery, appeared.

Alarmed, Verity opened her mouth and called for help.

At almost the same time Verity, Lady Hyacinth, and Lord Davies had first arrived at Vauxhall, the Marquess of Carrisworth had entered the gardens looking satanic. His hellish mood had nothing to do with seeing Miss Pymbroke riding off with Lord Davies. No, he told himself. He was no longer in the grip of jealousy that had sent him to his club to become foxed. That little episode over his frustrating landlady, so out of character for him, he chalked up to his body being unused to sobriety. He was quite himself again—carefree and in absolute control of his emotions.

Another matter was currently making him feel nettled. He had made the fatal mistake of going to Roxanna after hours of heavy drinking. Nothing had happened, and looking back on it now, he decided it had been simply boredom that had led him to her house.

In any event, the woman had clung to him like ivy ever since. For some incomprehensible reason, Roxanna had insisted on personally returning him to the house in South Audley Street, and had then remained with him, despite several broad hints to the contrary, once he had regained clear thinking. His temper had been tried beyond measure by the cunning actress's blatant desire to reestablish herself as his mistress. Finally, he had decided that taking her out would be the only way of eventually ridding himself of her that night.

"Perry, darling, did you send a servant ahead to reserve a box?" Roxanna's arm tightened on his and her blue eyes were like sapphires in the dark.

"Yes, though what Rupert will say if news of this outing reaches his ears, I cannot think. I would not countenance the defection of any lady under my protection," the marquess answered resolutely, guiding her in the lamplight toward the South Walk. He led her into a large box, which was decorated with paintings, and ordered ham and champagne.

"I swear I don't care what the duke knows, darling," she whispered, reaching across and placing her fingers on top of his. "I am the happiest of women when we are together and long to be joined as we once were."

The marquess took his gaze from the invitation in her eyes. And found his friend, Sir Ramsey, at the entrance to his box. "Randy, well met. Do join us," he said in a relieved voice.

Roxanna's lips thinned at this intrusion.

Sir Ramsey gave the actress a brief bow and entered the box, signaling to a waiter for another glass. He sighed heavily. "I tell you, Perry, I've had the most devilish luck this night. I was engaging in a bit of dalliance on the Dark Walk, and right when things were getting interesting, the lady was pulled from my arms by an outraged relative."

"You have my sympathy," the marquess said and grinned wolfishly.

Sir Ramsey drained his glass, noticing the frustrated expression on Roxanna's face. "Hey, now, I'm not playing gooseberry here, am I?"

"No, not at all. I am glad to see you," Lord Carrisworth answered, ignoring Roxanna's obvious anger. He sat back in his chair to relax, but immediately leaned forward, staring at the woman who'd appeared in front of them. A quick and disturbing thought presented itself in his brain.

"Good evening, Lord Carrisworth. How delightful to see you. Randy, I'm ready to leave now." Louisa patted her pale blonde hair, totally at her ease after leaving her sister alone to be ravaged. She ignored Roxanna, seeing at once the woman was beneath her notice.

Sir Ramsey rose. "We're off then."

As if holding a raw emotion in check, the marquess spoke stiffly. "Mrs. Barrington, is your sister here?"

A chill black silence ensued until, at last, Louisa found her voice. "Yes, Mouse, is with, er, a friend." Looking into Lord Carrisworth's knowing green eyes, she felt as if a hand had closed over her throat. A nervous laugh escaped her.

"Where is she?" the marquess's voice was icy.

Grabbing Sir Ramsey's arm, Louisa pulled him from the box. "The Dark Walk, my lord," she babbled, anxious to get away from what she feared might grow into a terrible scene.

But she need not have worried. At her words, Lord

Carrisworth bolted out of the box shouting, "Take Roxanna home, Randy!" and, not waiting to see how Louisa would react to the insult of being conveyed in the same vehicle as an actress, raced down the walkway, deftly avoiding the couples strolling there.

Meanwhile, Lord Davies, lounging against a tree, had heard Verity's cry for help. He made a move in her direction, then frowned. Perhaps it was not Miss Pymbroke's voice he'd heard call out in distress after all. He ran a hand through his wiry red hair and considered the matter. A few seconds later, he decided that, indeed, it was most probably Miss Pymbroke's voice, but, still, there was no sense risking his boots for any female.

Then he heard a strong masculine voice coming from somewhere to his right. "Miss Pymbroke! 'Tis I, Carrisworth. Where are you? Miss Pymbroke!"

Lord Davies's brain worked quickly. Here was his opportunity to further Roxanna's plan. Thinking ruefully of his precious boots, he plunged down the path and moments later, came upon the scene.

The three drunken bloods of the ton were taunting Verity. She had scrambled to her feet, with her back to the shrubbery, and was defending herself by kicking wildly at anyone who came close. One young man was clutching his leg while howling in pain.

At Lord Davies's appearance, they apparently decided to look for easier sport, and with a few final suggestions as to what the gentleman could do with the lady, they ran off.

Lord Davies successfully hid his disgust. His manner all solicitous, he extended a hand to Verity. "Miss Pymbroke, are you all right?"

Verity accepted his hand and stepped forward shakily. Her eyes were still glazed with fear. "Lord Davies, thank heavens you arrived when you did. I do not know how much longer I could hold them off." Her words ended with a tiny sob.

The baron put an arm around her shoulders to support her. Gad, when would Carrisworth find them? "I am all admiration at your bravery, dearest girl."

Allowing him to keep his arm about her, Verity looked up at him. "I am not so brave, sir. I confess to feeling a trifle wobbly."

Hearing the sounds of footsteps pounding down the walkway, Lord Davies pulled Verity closer and kissed her full on the mouth.

Sagging against him, Verity could not believe what was happening. Too shocked to move, she remained passive in his arms.

And that is how the marquess saw her, locked in Lord Davies's arms, a seemingly willing participant to his lovemaking.

Chapter Eight

It was late. Thick bands of fog invaded Vauxhall, casting the scene on the Dark Walk in a murky yellow.

"Davies, it appears you have won the lady after all. I suppose I should not have warned you off that day in the Green Room," the Marquess of Carrisworth drawled. His lazy voice was a contradiction to the blazing anger in his eyes.

Verity was barely aware of Lord Carrisworth's arrival. She freed herself from the baron by pushing against his chest with all her might. Her eyes filled with tears of frustration and humiliation. "How dare you, sirrah?"

Lord Davies looked from Miss Pymbroke's outraged face to the marquess's dangerous expression. He evidently viewed the lady as less likely to do injury to his person. "Forgive me, my dear. You led me to believe my attentions would not be unwelcome." With this whopping great lie, he made a jerking bow and disappeared into the fog.

Verity stared after him, unable to believe her ears. And only this morning, her trust in him had grown to the point where she accepted his escort on a drive to the Park.

"How fickle you are, Miss Pymbroke," Lord Carrisworth said. "And how our roles have reversed. Here I am having to remind you of the impropriety of bestowing your kisses haphazardly, while you behave like a light-skirt . . . or perhaps I should say like your sister. It must run in the family."

Verity stood very still. While she was certain he had not meant to, the marquess's words made her think of her father. She raised her eyes to him and the tears she had held rigidly in check coursed down her cheeks. "I-I *never* encouraged Lord Davies. He saved me from th-three odious young men wh-who were . . . and then he . . . oh!"

The marquess produced a large handkerchief and handed it to her. The sight of her small figure tormented, and clearly scandalized, gave him pause. But wait. Had not his mother always resorted to tears when his father had grown angry with her?

Uncertain what to believe, he stood irresolute. Part of him wanted to drag Miss Pymbroke into his arms and comfort her, but the other part dearly did not. Bitterly, he realized it was easy enough for him to draw a female into his arms for seduction, but now under the influence of tender emotions he felt frozen.

He saw she was drying her eyes and attempting to regain her composure, assuming a saintly mien, which was rather marred by a reddened nose.

"I had forgot," she said. "You are too self-absorbed to think of anyone else's feelings, and you have none your-self," she declared as one stating a plain truth.

The marquess felt himself relax. Of course his prim landlady would not have permitted Lord Davies to kiss her. Nor would she lie. He would have something to say to the baron on the morrow. The dastard.

He reached out and tenderly smoothed a curl from her face. "You amaze me, my avenging angel," he told her and pressed his hand to his heart. "I am all feeling. In truth, it would please me to show you, but, with what you have been through tonight, if I did so I would prove a coarse creature indeed."

"Thank you! You are all that is kind." To further her irritation, he suddenly chuckled. She longed to hit him. "If you would be so good to help me, my lord, I must find Lady Hyacinth."

Lord Carrisworth raised a dark eyebrow. "Why was Lady Hyacinth not with you?"

Verity looked down at her slippers as if they were the most interesting thing in the world. In a low voice she explained. "The servants told me Louisa had gone to Vauxhall with Sir Ramsey. I felt I needed to find her, and Lady Hyacinth offered to come with me. Lord Davies escorted us. When we arrived, I saw Louisa with Sir Ramsey and I followed them. That is when I was separated from Lady Hyacinth."

The marquess felt he could imagine Mrs. Barrington's anger at the interruption. But to leave her sister alone on the notorious Dark Walk—strumpet!

"Come, Miss Pymbroke," he said, adjusting the black gauze mantle about her shoulders and then offering her his arm. "We shall no doubt find Lady Hyacinth indulging in some of Vauxhall's famous ham and rack punch."

She accepted his arm and smiled up at him.

Lord Carrisworth's heart swelled with an emotion he had not thought himself capable of. He brutally pushed the feeling aside.

They searched for Lady Hyacinth for almost half an hour, the increasingly thick fog hampering their efforts. Finally, they came upon her ladyship, seated in a box with Lord Killigrew, tucking into a large helping of ham. The elderly lord's bulldog face was sulky because he had been unable to budge Lady Hyacinth away from her food so he might steal a kiss.

Lady Hyacinth waved her fork at them. "There you are, Verity, dear child. Oh, you are with Lord Carrisworth. That's all right and tight then."

They took their leave of Lord Killigrew, and her ladyship babbled on about Vauxhall all the way home in the marquess's Town coach, never once questioning the whereabouts of Lord Davies.

Both Lord Carrisworth and Verity were quiet on the way home.

Verity was tired and upset over the events of the evening. Upon arriving home, she was relieved to find Lady Iris had not yet returned from the Grahams' musicale.

Betty helped her mistress into a scanty lace shift, informing her anxiously that she had somehow lost one of miss's red silk garters. Verity dismissed her concern with a yawn. Exhaustion overcame her and she was asleep the minute her head rested upon the pillow.

Next door, lying in Verity's bed under her pink coverlet, the marquess was not so fortunate. He stared up at the pink and white bed hangings, unable to sleep.

Mr. Wetherall had been frosty upon his return. The servant's eye twitched convulsively as he reminded his master of the indiscretion he had committed by bringing Roxanna Hollings into the house. Furthermore, when he had taken his lordship's morning coat belowstairs to be brushed, he had been shocked to find a lady's red silk garter in the pocket.

The marquess had snatched the scrap of silk from the valet's fingers and tossed it onto the dressing table, curtly dismissing the servant for the night.

Only after he was alone did he allow his thoughts to return to his feelings for Miss Pymbroke. No, it would not do. He was not the man for her, even though he judged she was not indifferent to him. She was too innocent, too good to align herself with such as he. Besides, he reminded himself firmly, he would never marry and subject himself to the random whims of a woman's heart.

The morning of the Tremaines' ball, Verity stood in the hall of Lady Iris and Lady Hyacinth's house. The dressmaker had just delivered her ball gown, the one Lady Iris had commissioned in gold silk.

"Oh, my lady, thank you. It is the most beautiful dress I have ever owned." Verity was struck with awe. The material shimmered like liquid gold. Gold silk roses, embroidered in gold thread, adorned the bodice, the tiny puffed sleeves, and the full hem.

Lady Iris eyed the gown critically and finally pronounced it acceptable. "Have you any jewelry to go with it, gel?"

Verity's eyes opened wide in delight. "Mama's hair combs, the ones set with yellow topaz stones, will be the very thing." Then, she frowned. "Only I am quite certain I left them in my dressing table next door. I suppose the marquess would not mind the intrusion if I sent Betty—"

A crafty look came into Lady Iris's eyes. "Betty is busy helping Beecham repair one of my gowns. Run next door yourself. You needn't worry about Carrisworth. I saw him ride off earlier." Lady Iris felt no need to tell her young friend she had also seen his lordship return some fifteen minutes ago. The two needed a bit of prodding, she thought impatiently. Lawks, it was already May. They should be announcing their betrothal by now!

Verity folded the gown and replaced it in the box. "I had better be quick then, before the marquess returns."

Placing the box on a nearby table, she went out the front door.

Lady Iris's face creased into a smile. She began climbing the stairs on her way to the drawing room when she saw Empress standing at the top of the stairs, gazing down at her. The cat's tail swayed back and forth sinuously, and the expression on her face was one of a coconspirator.

Reaching her pet, Lady Iris bent down and scratched Empress's crowned head. "Not quite as drastic as burning down his townhouse, but with any luck, it might prove interesting."

Had Lady Iris but known it, she had yet another cohort in her plans for the marquess and Verity. Mr. Wetherall happened to be passing through the hall when Verity knocked. He opened the door wide and recognized her at once. "Good morning, Miss Pymbroke. I am Mr. Wetherall, Lord Carrisworth's valet. May I be of assistance?"

"Thank you, Mr. Wetherall," Verity said, entering the house. "I do not wish to disturb anyone. It is only that I have left something in my dressing table I wish to retrieve. I understand his lordship is away from home, so I thought I might just run up and get it."

A good servant knew how to keep his expression a perfect blank. "Of course, miss. Please go ahead."

Verity smiled at the old man and then hurried up the stairs.

Mr. Wetherall raised a shaking, veined hand to his brow. Never had he been so blind to the conventions. But, he told himself, the circumstance of seeing that actress Roxanna Hollings in the house yesterday had driven him to extreme measures. He staggered under the weight of his duplicity down to the butler's sitting room, where he was sure a glass of wine would restore his equanimity.

Upstairs, after throwing open the door to her old bed-chamber, Verity quickly crossed the room to the dressing table. Abruptly, she stopped short, staring down at her missing red silk garter resting on the smooth surface. "How on earth—"

"So, Empress was correct. It is yours," a lazy voice drawled.

Verity whirled around. The Marquess of Carrisworth lounged in a bath situated in a corner not ten feet away. His manner did not indicate any uneasiness at finding himself stark naked in the presence of a lady. Instead, his face held an expression of unholy amusement.

Verity's breath caught in her lungs. She stared, saucer-eyed, and tried to speak, but could not. How muscular his chest and shoulders were! Oh! She must not look. But, unbelievably, she could not stop herself.

"I must say, Miss Pymbroke," he said casually, ignoring her confusion and discomfort, "my imagination ran rampant when Empress brought me your garter. Tell me, why does such a proper young lady possess *such* an enticing piece of silk?" His green eyes sparkled.

Ooooh! Empress and her ribbon fetish. How dare the marquess mention . . . this was insupportable. Verity made as if to move toward the door.

Lord Carrisworth placed both hands on the sides of the huge copper basin and slowly began to rise. "If you try to leave before you have answered my question, I shall stand up."

Verity froze. Averting her head, she answered him in a stilted voice. "If you must know, I enjoy feminine under-garments, my lord. Please, I merely came here for some combs I left in my dressing table. I thought you were out riding."

The marquess waved a hand negligently, causing some water to splash on the floor, but his gaze never left her. "Ah, red silk. I knew all along you were a romantic. But, please, do not let me distract you from your task."

A naked gentleman a distraction? Verity felt a nervous giggle rise in her throat. Suppressing it, she turned around awkwardly. While doing so, her treacherous gaze rested for a moment on the light covering of dark hair across his lordship's chest. A new and unexpected warmth surged through her. Confused and shaking, she turned away. Snatching the garter from the table, she jerked open the drawer and grabbed the combs.

Clutching the articles in a trembling hand, she averted her gaze from his lordship and dashed for the door. Racing down the hallway, her cheeks burning, she heard the marquess's laughter. There was no sign of Mr. Wetherall downstairs—never again would she place the slightest confidence in *him*—and, so, she let herself out, mercifully unnoticed.

Bursting into the hall of Lady Iris and Lady Hyacinth's, Verity came face to face with Cynthia, Countess of Northbridge, who was handing Bingwood her card. The butler said, "There you are, miss. I was just going to say you were not at home. Lady Iris informed me you had gone next door to the Marquess of Carrisworth's house."

The countess raised an elegant eyebrow and gazed speculatively at her new friend. "Why, Verity, you are looking overset. Have I called at an inopportune time?"

Verity gathered her shaken wits. She crammed the combs and the garter in her pocket. Dismissing the butler, she held out both hands to her guest saying, "Not at all, Cynthia. In fact, I had hoped to see you yesterday."

"Do forgive me," the countess begged, accepting Verity's outstretched hands and giving them an affectionate squeeze. She lowered her voice to a whisper. "I hope you are not offended by plain speaking. You see, I was with the physician, hoping he would confirm my suspicions that I might soon be providing Charles with the heir he longs for. But, alas, the doctor said he did not believe me to be with child."

"Oh, I am so sorry."

The countess shook her head and smiled. "Do not be. It is my experience that women know more about these things than even the doctors. It is early days and I still have hope. Now, I did not come here to talk of myself. I hear Perry is to escort you and the Ladies Iris and Hyacinth to the Tremaines' ball this evening. Charles and I are going as well. We shall have such fun."

Verity tried to hide her dismay from Cynthia's intelligent gaze. How could she face the marquess again so soon after this morning's embarrassing episode? Pasting a smile on her face, she said, "I am glad to hear you will be attending. But, you must think me rag-mannered, indeed. Let us go up to the drawing room for some tea. We can discuss the ball there."

"Yes, and I shall show you the steps of the waltz. It is most romantic," Cynthia assured her.

The two women linked arms and climbed the stairs. Each was busy with her own thoughts.

At Cynthia's offer, Verity's mind flashed back to the night of the Lexhams' turtle dinner when the marquess had "waltzed" with her in the hall. Really, he had done no more than hold her in his arms, so Cynthia's instruction would be welcome. What was not welcome was the memory of the warm feelings Lord Carrisworth had roused in her that night . . . as well as only moments ago.

After seeing his lordship in his bath, Verity could not banish the vision of the marquess's bare chest from her brain. It seemed every encounter with him left her dizzy with an emotion she could not name. Well, that was not exactly true. Certainly she could name annoyance and frustration. But underneath them was this other feeling. The one that frightened her. The one she closed her mind to as she led the countess upstairs.

The Countess of Northbridge was thinking that if Verity had really, as the butler had indicated, come from Perry's house, it was fascinating intelligence indeed. The girl's cheeks had been quite pink. What could be going on?

While Perry liked to give the impression he was a rattle, Cynthia had long ago determined he had a code of honor as strict as any gentleman. Never would he seduce a young innocent like Verity. Which meant his interest in her must be serious. How wonderful it would be for Charles's best friend to finally settle down. She could hardly wait to see them together tonight so she might judge for herself.

Impeccably garbed in a dark brown evening coat over a white waistcoat and cream-colored knee breeches, the Marquess of Carrisworth stood in Lady Iris's drawing room waiting for Miss Pymbroke.

He had greeted the ladies warmly, with the exception of Mrs. Barrington, to whom he gave only a chilly nod. The widow, striking in a ruby-colored gown with ruby stones at her ears and neck, had ground her teeth at the slight.

Lady Hyacinth was wrapped in a colorful cashmere shawl and was sipping wine and munching a biscuit.

Lady Iris was clad in an old-fashioned hooped gown of a dark green color. Beneath her high white wig, her face was covered in its usual white paint, and she wore a heart-shaped patch by her mouth. "I don't know what's keeping Verity," she fibbed. For Lady Iris had given strict instructions to Beecham to delay the girl's arrival downstairs so she might make an entrance in front of Carrisworth.

Then, Bingwood opened the double doors and Verity stood framed in the doorway. As Lady Iris had known it would, the gold-colored gown set off Verity's figure and coloring to perfection. Her hair had been fashioned into an elegant style with curls falling from her mother's jeweled combs. Long white gloves encased her arms, and a slim gold chain encircled her neck. Her velvet-brown eyes shone with excitement, the preparations for the ball pushing aside her fears of meeting the marquess again. "I do apologize for keeping everyone waiting. Beecham would not stop fussing over my hair."

When she entered the room, Lord Carrisworth thought he had never seen her more beautiful. He deliberately let his gaze travel down her body. "Miss Pymbroke—" he began, but broke off as an arrested expression came over his face.

Bowing to the ladies, he said, "Excuse me for just one moment, please."

He walked quickly out the door while everyone looked at one another in confusion. In a few short minutes he returned, and walked directly to Verity.

Standing close to her, he could smell her rose perfume. "For this one night, you must forget Society's rule regarding the nature of a gift a gentleman may give a lady. When I saw these, I knew they were meant for only you."

Paying no attention to the bewildered expression on Verity's face, he reached out and clasped a yellow topaz eardrop on first one ear, then the other. Staring into her startled eyes, he whispered, "You truly are an angel, my landlady."

Seeming to recall where he was, he stepped back and moved away rather quickly. He poured himself a glass of wine.

"Oh," gasped Lady Hyacinth. "Dear child, the yellow topaz matches your Mama's combs and is ideal with your hair and gown." She and Lady Iris exchanged optimistic glances.

Verity stood too emotion-filled to speak. The touch of Lord Carrisworth's firm fingers against the softness of her neck and ears had caused an intense craving to fill her body. She had wanted him to pull her into his arms then and there. That he had thought of her, had purchased something simply because he judged it would compliment her, sent her spirits soaring. For a moment her strict observation of the rules of Society battled with her growing feelings for the marquess.

Her heart won. She walked over to the mirror and viewed the beautiful eardrops. "Thank you, my lord. I shall agree to forgo the conventions for tonight."

"What a relief for us all, I'm sure," Louisa said derisively.

Verity's happiness crumbled. She turned away from the glass and stared at the carpet. Her sister had avoided her assiduously since Vauxhall, giving the impression she wanted nothing further to do with her. Verity felt the loss acutely.

Lord Carrisworth eyed the widow with dislike.

Suddenly, Louisa let out a shrill cry. "The monster! Look what that horrible animal has done to my gown!"

All eyes turned to where Empress, with a length of ruby-colored ribbon dangling from her mouth, sat wearing an expression that defied anyone to challenge her royal catliness. She had obviously unwound the ribbon from the hem of Louisa's gown.

Lady Iris barked a laugh. She bent and, from long experience, retrieved the ribbon easily. "Empress, what are we to do with you," she scolded halfheartedly.

"I can tell you," Louisa said, her gray eyes like granite. "A trip to the river with a stone tied around its neck is what that cat needs."

As one, the company glared at Louisa in disapproval. The marquess raised his quizzing glass and studied her. "You know, Mrs. Barrington, in ancient Egypt the penalty for killing a cat was death."

"Makes good sense to me," Lady Iris responded roundly. "And what's more, I ain't going to wait while Beecham repairs that gown or you decide to change. You can send a message to one of your flirts to escort you to the Tremaines'. Come along, Carrisworth, let us take our leave."

Verity hesitated but a moment before following the others.

Empress trailed after them downstairs. Lady Iris left orders for her pet to be given a dish of cream in the kitchens and kept there until she returned from the ball. "Not that Louisa would dare harm a hair on Empress, but the servants tend to coddle the cat and she'll be better off there than alone while I'm gone."

The marquess and Verity exchanged a look behind Lady Iris's back which clearly expressed the view in both their minds that Lady Iris herself had spoiled Empress. They shared a smile.

Despite the unpleasantness with Louisa, it was a jovial

party that rode in the utmost luxury in Lord Carrisworth's traveling coach. The Duke and Duchess of
Tremaine were holding their party at their manor house,
which was a few miles outside of London, and the marquess believed the distance was best covered in comfort.
He served the ladies wine from a sort of cupboard fixed
in one side of the coach and amused them with the latest
on dits.

In the dim light inside the coach, Verity thought it
wickedly unjust that the marquess should appear so
handsome. Her fingers moved to caress the eardrops he
had given—no, lent—her. While she had agreed to
ignore the conventions for this night, she would return
the jewelry in the morning. With a sigh she realized she
would do so with no small amount of regret.

A short time later, the coach wound its way down a
long, curving drive. The large, sprawling manor house
built in the Elizabethan style that sprang into view was an
awesome reflection of power and prestige.

Lady Iris peered out of the coach window. "By
George, this promises to be the greatest possible fun. The
Duchess of Tremaine is holding the party on the roof!"

Verity gasped in delight. "Oh, what a wonderful idea."

"Bless me," Lady Hyacinth moaned, her plump hands
flying to her cheeks. "I have the most dreadful fear of
heights."

"For God's sake then, Hyacinth, don't look over the
edge," her sister instructed her crossly.

A footman accompanied them when they made their
way through the grand house and up the stairs, lit by
torches.

The duchess had ordered thick Oriental carpets to be
laid on the rooftop. Stands of hothouse flowers were
spread about, and cloth-covered tables held mountains of

refreshments. A small orchestra played near a larger area that was being used for dancing. Bordering the roof were large stone pillars, turrets, and gargoyles. Above it all, the black sky presented a brilliant backdrop of glowing stars and a full moon.

Lady Hyacinth looked around her wide-eyed. Lord Carrisworth placed an affectionate arm about her shoulders and said, "You see, my lady, there are footmen stationed two feet apart, like guards, around the perimeter of the roof so you may be secure."

Lady Hyacinth nodded. Gentlemen were so reassuring. "I suspect they are there to prevent tipsy guests from stumbling to their deaths. It does provide one with a great sense of safety."

Lady Iris grabbed her arm. "Come on. Let's find the duke and duchess."

As they made their way over to where the Tremaines were greeting guests, Verity gazed up at the handsome marquess and smiled. He had handled Lady Hyacinth's fears gallantly. Indeed, his lordship seemed full of consideration for others this night. Could it be he was not the care-for-nobody she had originally judged him?

The Duke of Tremaine was a crabby old man of at least seventy years. In contrast, his wife was a thirtyish, vibrant woman with auburn hair who gazed at Lord Carrisworth with hungry eyes. Introductions were performed, and Verity curtsyed low. She watched gloomily while the marquess flirted expertly with the duchess.

The musicians struck up a waltz. Verity turned and found Beau Brummell, faultlessly attired in evening dress, at her side. He bowed to the ladies and nodded at Lord Carrisworth. "Miss Pymbroke, I have obtained permission for you to waltz from Lady Cowper, one of the patronesses of Almack's. And you did promise me a dance." He held out his arm expectantly.

Verity accepted him with a backward glance at the marquess. Why could it not be Lord Carrisworth to twirl her about the floor? She then flushed, realizing the marquess was watching her with that teasing twinkle in his green eyes.

Firmly pushing thoughts of Lord Carrisworth from her mind, she devoted herself to her conversation with Mr. Brummell and their dance. They exchanged pleasantries and then he said, "The duchess has a marvelous sense of style. When she realized the unusually warm weather was perfect for an outdoor party, she immediately ordered everything moved to the roof. Charming, is it not?"

"Yes," Verity replied distractedly. Her disobedient gaze had returned to the marquess who was leading the duchess out onto the floor. Verity felt her stomach knot when Lord Carrisworth placed a gloved hand at the lady's waist.

Mr. Brummell was not aware he had less than a captive audience. "Our dear duchess is a romantic, and what could be more suitable for intrigue and stolen kisses than a night under the stars?"

Verity bit her lip as the lady laughed at something Lord Carrisworth had whispered into her ear. "Indeed," she replied faintly.

"There was already a bit of excitement before you arrived. Lady Althea announced her engagement."

Mr. Brummell had Verity's attention now. In the most casual way she glanced around the company searching for the long-nosed Lady Althea. Although she knew the answer, she asked, "Pray, to whom is the lady engaged?"

"Cecil Sedgewick, an aspiring cleric. The Foxworths

have given him a living. Lady Althea appears happy with her choice, and I believe it will be best for her. She is rather a domineering sort and Sedgewick seems willing enough to be under the cat's paw."

Verity spotted the couple in question. Mr. Sedgewick was solicitously adjusting a shawl around his fiancée's shoulders. For the first time, Verity realized what a hypocrite Cecil Sedgewick was. Oh, how he had pontificated on the evils of Society and the uncaring members of the Nobility! Yet here he was, engaged to one of its most pampered daughters. Lord Carrisworth had been correct regarding Mr. Sedgewick's motivations. Well, Mr. Sedgewick had what he wanted now, and Verity wished Lady Althea the joy of him. That she had ever considered him desirable as a husband made her shudder.

"You are not cold, are you, Miss Pymbroke?" Mr. Brummell inquired. The dance had ended and they were strolling toward Lady Iris.

"No, thank you for asking, Mr. Brummell."

The Beau left her with a bow. Lady Iris tapped a closed fan against the palm of her hand while gazing about the gathering. "There is your slut of a sister. She got Sir Ramsey to bring her here. Pah! She's wasting her time on him. There's no hope in that direction. The man's too smart for her. You know, I can't seem to find Hyacinth."

Verity took note of Louisa, hanging on Sir Ramsey's arm, and then looked at Lady Iris in surprise. "My lady, could Lady Hyacinth have not simply, er, retired to the ladies withdrawing room for a moment?"

"Perhaps. But she was with Lord Killigrew and I don't like him. He looks like a dog on the hunt for a bone." Her ladyship raised her fan and pointed it at Lord Carrisworth commandingly.

The marquess bowed to the duchess and came to their side, a brow raised in inquiry.

"Carrisworth, Hyacinth's missing. I want you to find her."

The marquess gazed at Lady Iris limpidly. "Missing? Did you look over the edge of the house?"

Lady Iris bridled. "This is no time for funning. Killigrew is with her, and I suspect while my back was turned the dirty dog whisked her away downstairs."

"Very well. Come, Miss Pymbroke, I may need your help." Before Verity could protest, he led her away without the slightest protest from Lady Iris.

They made their way back down the torch-lit stairs. When they reached the bottom, Lord Carrisworth paused for a moment to study her. "Have you heard the news about your Mr. Sedgewick? Is your heart broken, Miss Pymbroke?"

Verity pursed her lips. Her brown eyes sparkled when she replied. "I wish them happy." Seeing the amused expression on his face she went on in a rush. "What do you want? For me to admit I was wrong about him and you were right?"

The marquess grinned wolfishly. "That would be pleasant. But I owe you an apology. I did not live up to my part of our bargain when we agreed I should help you catch Mr. Sedgewick for yourself. I do most humbly beg your pardon."

"Fudge! You are not in the slightest bit sorry," she told him.

He acknowledged the truth of this with a nod of his head. "He was not the man for you, my landlady. You have too much spirit for a dull cleric. And one who does not live up to his principles."

Verity contemplated the sculpture atop a marble base

in the hall where they were standing. In a low voice she said, "It seems I have been a poor judge of people. First, Mr. Sedgewick, then Louisa—"

"And me, Miss Pymbroke. Why, I am all sincerity, and on many occasions you have called my integrity into question."

Verity straightened her shoulders. A discussion of the marquess's character was not one she wished to enter into when her own thoughts on the subject were so perplexing. "We are supposed to be locating Lady Hyacinth."

They walked down the hall and peered into the library, then a saloon, and Verity investigated the ladies withdrawing room, all to no avail. Retracing their steps, they encountered Sir Ramsey approaching them from the roof stairs. "I'm for White's, Perry. Care to join me?"

"No, my friend. But why are you leaving so early?"

Sir Ramsey glanced uncomfortably at Verity. "Forgive me, Miss Pymbroke, but it's your sister. Don't know what maggot she's taken into her head. I swear I never gave her any indication I was the marrying type. Deuced uncomfortable business, but Louisa knows the way the wind blows now and she's not happy. Thought it best to take my leave."

Sir Ramsey moved past them. Verity's mind raced. Her sister must have brought up the subject of marriage to the baronet and he had denied her just as Lady Iris had guessed he would. Poor Louisa!

Lord Carrisworth read her mind. He grasped her arm in a tight hold. "Miss Pymbroke, you cannot be thinking charitably of your sister after the events at Vauxhall. You just admitted you had been wrong about Mrs. Barrington. Confound it, you are an intelligent girl! Realize her way of life is not compatible with yours and you cannot change her."

Tears formed in Verity's eyes. "Yes. I shall let her go her own way. I saw last night I have no choice." She raised pain-filled eyes to his. "Tell me, my lord, why is it that people we love often hurt us so much?"

The marquess caught his breath. He pulled Verity into his arms. She rested her head on his shoulder and he stroked her back gently. His jaw had tensed, and he had a faraway expression in his green eyes. "We give them that power by loving them."

Verity eased out of his hold. Brown eyes stared into green. "You speak as if from experience. Did someone you love hurt you?"

Lord Carrisworth turned away to adjust the sleeve of his coat. When he looked at her again, his face betrayed no emotion. Verity had a sudden urge to shake him.

From the other end of the hall came the sound of muffled weeping. As one, the marquess and Verity hurried to its source.

Chapter Nine

Lord Carrisworth and Verity reached an anteroom they had previously failed to explore. Lady Hyacinth reclined in a half-swoon on a red velvet sofa, her hand to her brow. A nervous Lord Killigrew was standing nearby. "It was nothing to fly up into the boughs over," he said, shifting his bulky weight from one foot to the other.

Verity crossed the room to the lady's side. "My lady, are you all right?"

Lady Hyacinth's eyes were round with fear. The woman who claimed to have had many amorous adventures with gentlemen cried out in anguish, "Merciful heavens, Verity, that terrible man kissed me!"

Lord Carrisworth hid a smile. Then he became aware of Miss Pymbroke's flashing brown eyes. His expression turned stern and he spoke coldly to Lord Killigrew. "Sir, I shall not insult Lady Hyacinth by asking you what your intentions are toward her. A lady of such spirit would never consign herself to a marriage with a dull dog like you."

Lord Killigrew's complexion paled, and his jowls shook as his mouth worked soundlessly.

A tiny cry escaped the spinster on the sofa, but she rallied under the marquess's next words.

"A beauty like Lady Hyacinth can have her pick of

suitors. It is unfortunate for us gentlemen that she has not deemed anyone worthy of her hand thus far, but that is her choice. You will not force your attentions on her again. Do I make myself clear?"

"Yes, my lord," Lord Killigrew replied, a bit too hastily. "So terribly sorry. No offense meant." He bowed himself out of the room and could be heard rapidly retreating down the hall.

Verity patted her ladyship's hand. Once she realized her friend was in no danger, she had been free to admire the masterful way Lord Carrisworth protected and flattered Lady Hyacinth while sending Lord Killigrew on his way. His gallantry, his concern for the older lady's sensibilities, touched her heart.

Lord Carrisworth came to the ladies and gazed down at Lady Hyacinth. He shook a finger and scolded, "My lady, you are heartless. You know a gentleman can only restrain himself in the presence of a lovely woman for so long before he succumbs to her charms."

Verity could not believe the sudden transformation of Lady Hyacinth's features. The older woman's red lips curved into a coy smile and her eyes danced merrily. She sat up on the sofa and allowed Lord Carrisworth to assist her to her feet. "Should I apologize to poor Lord Killigrew?" her ladyship asked while adjusting a shawl about her shoulders.

Lord Carrisworth's shoulders shook, and Verity shot him a warning glance. "Nonsense, my lady. The matter is best forgotten," she said.

But it was kept very much alive by Lady Hyacinth herself when the trio returned to the party on the roof. She immediately rushed over to where Lady Iris was seated with three other ladies of a certain age and proceeded to boast of her latest conquest.

Lady Iris was clearly out-of-sorts upon hearing the story. While the other ladies gasped in dismay and fanned themselves vigorously relishing every detail of Lady Hyacinth's "seduction," Lady Iris took a large pinch of snuff—Violet Strasburg, Queen Charlotte's favorite—and declared it was all just another of Hyacinth's fancies.

Lady Hyacinth hotly denied any exaggeration of the matter, and the two sisters were off and running with one of their famous quarrels.

Lord Carrisworth turned to Verity. "I think we may safely leave them. Ah, I hear the strains of a waltz. May I have the pleasure, my landlady?"

Verity shyly accepted his arm and they joined the other dancers. The Earl of Northbridge held his Cynthia, pretty in turquoise silk, as, totally engrossed in each other, they swept past.

The marquess placed his gloved hand at the hollow of Verity's spine. His other hand came up to hold hers, and they swirled into the steps of the dance. Under the stars he twirled her around, the golden topaz eardrops shimmering against the creamy white of her neck.

As he looked down at her, Perry thought she had never appeared more like an angel. A light breeze wafted over them, and he could smell her rose perfume. Her body was warm and pliant under his hands and her hair shone. He felt there was an almost unbearable sweetness about her.

It would be a small step to fall in love with her.

Lord Carrisworth pulled back slightly and placed another two inches between his body and Miss Pymbroke's. He could not allow his thoughts to travel down that sort of dangerous path. Good God, the small step it would take to fall in love with Miss Pymbroke would be tantamount to the small step it would take to fall off this roof!

He realized he had been staring down into her pansy brown eyes for most of the dance without uttering a word. He cleared his throat and said, "I have not been able to run Lord Davies to earth. It is being said in the clubs he was publicly accused of cheating at cards and has not been seen since. Rest assured, though, I intend to take him to task for his behavior toward you at Vauxhall."

At his words, Verity slowly exhaled. The marquess had been looking at her with a tenderness and an affection that had stopped her breath. Now the wonderful warm feeling his gaze had elicited dimmed. "You need not trouble yourself, my lord. I doubt Lord Davies will call on me again, but if he does, I confess I should like an explanation from him as to why he kissed me."

The marquess looked at her skeptically and drawled, "Come now, Miss Pymbroke, you plan to demand a *reason*?" He shook his head and chuckled.

The last notes of the music died. The marquess and Verity were standing near a large stone turret. Suddenly, there was a loud shrieking sound and the black sky exploded with color. The duchess was providing her guests with a brilliant display of fireworks.

Startled by the sudden noise, Verity clung to Lord Carrisworth's arm.

He was acutely conscious of the pressure of her small hand. Trying desperately to suppress his feelings, he said, "The duchess has thought of everything. But you have not answered me, my landlady. What explanation could Lord Davies give other than he was enchanted by you?"

Verity felt a wave of frustration like she had never

experienced before. Was he humoring *her* the way he had Lady Hyacinth a short time ago? "You odious man, can you never cease your flirting and be serious?"

The teasing twinkle left Lord Carrisworth's eyes. He pulled Verity around the other side of the stone turret away from view. "Certainly I can be serious. Allow me to show you," he replied, and crushed her against his chest.

His lips came down on hers in just the sort of kiss a rake would bestow on one of his paramours. It was a cold, hard, practiced kiss meant to exact a response from her.

A small whimper came from Verity's throat, and the marquess immediately drew back. He saw her brown eyes were huge in her face reflecting her hurt and bewilderment.

The Marquess of Carrisworth felt something deep inside him snap.

He lowered his dark head and began pressing very light, soft kisses on her face. First her forehead, then her eyelids, the tip of her nose, until finally his lips hovered above her trembling mouth.

He raised a shaking hand to cradle the back of her head while his lips met hers with a surprisingly gentle touch. This time, the kiss was more of a caress which deepened until his mouth pressed harder and then began moving across her lips.

Verity shivered at his tenderness, and when the pressure of his lips increased, she felt her mouth burn. A searing passion raced through her and she kissed him back with a hunger so intense that she felt faint.

Lord Carrisworth was lost in a world where Miss Pymbroke's lips were the most delicious delicacy he had ever tasted. His hand at her waist pressed her ever closer to him so that her breasts were pushed against his white waistcoat. His thumb moved in circles against the small of her back in the familiar gesture he often used on her hand.

From a great distance his lordship heard someone give a loud cough. With a Herculean effort he raised his head from the drugging sweetness of Miss Pymbroke's lips, noting they were red and swollen. He looked around. Charles, the Earl of Northbridge, and his wife were standing next to the turret. Charles had a worried expression on his face. Cynthia was grinning.

Verity felt her face flame. She slowly pulled away from Lord Carrisworth's embrace because he had forgotten to let her go. She raised a hand and attempted to tidy her hair, avoiding everyone's gaze. Her heart was hammering painfully in her chest and the bottom of her stomach ached.

Charles broke the silence. He fixed his disapproving gaze on his friend and spoke somewhat stiffly. "The fireworks have ended, and Cynthia and I are going to take our leave. We just wanted to say hello."

"And goodbye," Cynthia added cheerfully. "A jolly party was it not, Perry? And, Verity dear, your gown is perfection. I shall call on you tomorrow." With that, she firmly led her husband away.

"And I shall call on you, Perry," Charles said over his shoulder.

Lord Carrisworth spoke for the first time, his voice husky. "I must return you to Lady Iris."

In a daze, Verity took the marquess's arm and they made their way to Lady Iris. That lady's sharp eyes rested on Verity's lips, but she said nothing. A niggling doubt about whether the marquess was serious troubled her ladyship part of the way home in the carriage. But, she reminded herself, Carrisworth had never toyed with an innocent young miss in the past. His heart was engaged, she was sure. Now if she could just depend upon him not to do anything rattle-headed. A large "if," for weren't gentlemen famous for want of sense? She was able to ponder these questions in peace because Lady Hyacinth, exhausted from the excitement of her conquest, promptly fell asleep as soon as the wheels of the coach began turning.

Lord Carrisworth considered feigning sleep, but rejected the idea in favor of staring out the coach window into the black night. He was overcome by a riot of emotions and needed time to sort them through. Alone. His feelings were so raw he could not bring himself to exchange pleasantries with Lady Iris or with the angel—nay, sorceress—sitting next to him. It was disturbing enough that the entire side of his body closest to Verity throbbed as if it were being pulled by an invisible magnet toward her. He moved as far away on his side of the seat as he could.

Verity was equally aware of him. Some of the lime scent he wore must have rubbed off on her glove as she had wound her arms about his neck during their embrace. She had only to raise her hand to stroke the eardrops he had given her to smell the light, pleasing scent.

Drawing in a deep breath and releasing it slowly, Verity clasped her hands in her lap and stared down at them. Tonight the marquess had shown her a side of his personality she instinctively knew no other woman had seen. He had been vulnerable to her, as she was to him. Verity had never felt so afraid. All her life she had determined not to fall in love. And what must she needs do but give her heart to a rake?

The heart in question abruptly felt as if it jumped from her chest into her throat. *She was not in love with Lord Carrisworth!* No, indeed not, she told herself firmly.

How could she be? She had only to remember what Papa had done to Mama.

The treacherous idea that Papa had never loved Mama presented itself in her thoughts. Her eyes filled with tears as she recognized this as the truth. Theirs had been a marriage of convenience. Mama had a large dowry, and Viscount Eldon had heavy gaming debts. But Mama had always told her the handsome viscount had been so charming she had thought that besides the money he had cared for her, but, alas, that had proven not to be the case.

Perhaps, a little voice in Verity's brain cried, Lord Carrisworth—Perry—was different. Perhaps he did love her. She bit her lip when the memory of the tenderness of his touch came rushing back. Was not his tenderness a sign of love? Oh, but what if it were only a fleeting passion? She could not be sure unless his lordship declared himself and until—if—that time came she would have to be strong and judge for herself if his feelings were genuine.

Late the next morning, Lord Carrisworth sat on the bench in the rose garden behind Verity's townhouse. The day was sunny with a brisk chill in the air. He had just returned from his morning ride, changed into a dark green morning coat and tan pantaloons, and was feeling burnt almost to the socket. He had spent a devilish bad night tossing and turning, trying to ignore the fact that every fiber of his being was calling out for Miss Pymbroke. No night spent drinking and gaming had ever left him this out of frame.

"Miaow." Empress jumped up on the seat beside him.

Lord Carrisworth reached out a hand to scratch Empress's crowned head. "You are looking content this morning, my feline friend. Treated you right last night in Lady Iris's kitchen, did they?"

The cat purred in answer.

Digby appeared at the glass doors to the morning room. "My lord, a Mr. Flanders has called. I believe he is with the company doing the restoration work on your lordship's family portraits."

The marquess rose to his feet. "Show him into the morning room, Digby."

Empress followed Lord Carrisworth through the open door into the house and promptly found a gold velvet-covered chair—the most comfortable in the room—and stretched out on its plump seat.

A moment later a thin, tall man with light hair entered with a servant who carried a painting wrapped in protective paper. "Good day to you, my lord. I am Mr. Flanders." He bowed low. "I thought your lordship would like to see some of the work I have done for you."

The marquess gave a nod of assent.

Mr. Flanders snapped his fingers at the servant who then unwrapped the painting.

Lord Carrisworth instantly felt a knot form in his stomach. He gritted his teeth and braced himself for the jolt of pain he still experienced every time he saw his mother's face.

"A beautiful lady," Mr. Flanders was saying while he propped the painting up against a chair. "It was a privilege to restore her portrait, my lord. Is she perhaps an older sister? Her emerald-colored gown appears to be a fashion of perhaps twenty years ago—"

"My mother," the marquess bit out tersely, cutting off the man's stream of chatter. "You have performed your services satisfactorily, Mr. Flanders. I trust you will repair the other paintings equally as well."

"Yes, my lord." Mr. Flanders blinked at this abrupt dismissal. "I shall just wrap the portrait and be on my way."

"Leave it," Lord Carrisworth commanded.

The two men bowed and left the morning room. The marquess left the portrait where it was and sat on the gold satin sofa opposite where the painting was placed. He stared at his mother's features, his own like granite.

Digby entered the room, drawing back a bit when he saw the look on his lordship's face. "I am sorry to disturb you, but Mr. Flanders said he found this in the back of the painting. He forgot to give it to you just now."

The butler extended a silver salver upon which sat a yellowed piece of parchment tied with a frayed blue ribbon.

The marquess accepted the missive and Digby left, closing the door behind him.

His expression hard and set, Lord Carrisworth tossed the unopened paper onto an occasional table placed at the end of the sofa. He had a strong feeling he did not wish to know its contents.

The very second the missive landed on the polished wood, Empress bounded from her chair, ran the length of the sofa, jumped across his lordship's lap and onto the table, which rocked ominously under the cat's weight. She pounced on the ribbons of the missive, grabbing one end in her dainty jaws, and dashed under the sofa with it before the marquess could do more than stare.

"For God's sake!" Lord Carrisworth got down on his knees and looked under the sofa. Empress crouched with the missive between her paws. Her slanted blue eyes challenged him.

The marquess was never one to walk away from a challenge. He lunged for the paper and took it away, managing to escape with only a minor scratch from Empress's sharp claws for his trouble. Empress materialized from under the sofa and walked, stiff with outrage at the loss of her toy, through the open door to the garden.

Lord Carrisworth returned to his seat on the sofa and stared down at the paper, which he now saw was addressed to him in a feminine handwriting. Slowly, he pushed the ribbon aside and opened the parchment. Noticing the letter was dated over thirteen years ago, he took a deep breath and began to read.

London, 14 April, 1800

My dear Perry—

I write this on the eve of the day I shall finally be able to be with the Gentleman I have loved since I was seventeen. No one in England knows of our Plans as we have been very careful not to be Found Out.

Allow me to begin at the beginning. During my first Season in London I fell Unalterably in Love with Nigel, and he with me. Before we could become betrothed, a Scheming woman named Josephine, who wanted Nigel for his title and money, managed to lure him under False Pretenses into the deserted Library at a Ball. He saw her Plan almost instantly but the lady was too clever for him. Her Mama conveniently came upon them and threatened a Scandal. My Nigel was forced to marry Josephine.

I was inconsolable. Not caring who I married, I agreed when my parents chose your father, Arthur. He was so much older than I, and I believed him a wise man.

Although not many people knew Nigel and I were in love, Arthur somehow heard. Immediately after our wedding, he took me away from my family and everyone I knew to live in his house in Yorkshire. It was a lonely existence. My first happy moment came two years later, my son, when you were born. At least one good thing had come of my marriage—you.

I spent the next seventeen years trying to please your father, but I do not think he ever got over the fact that I had been in love with another man. You know, my dear, he could be Fearsome when he was angry. He often Forbade me from even seeing you, feeling it best you were raised by Nurse and later your Tutor. Then you were sent away to Eton. I often felt we had never been allowed to become Close. But know, Perry, that I have always Loved you.

Arthur finally brought me back to London one month ago. He wished you to see the Town before going to Oxford. At the very first party we attended I met Nigel. My dear, it was as if the almost twenty years in between had never happened. Of course, many things had changed. Before she died, Josephine had given him a daughter who was now grown and married to an army man. Nigel, thinking me lost to him Forever, as well as being Deeply in Debt, had married again and they have a little girl who is six years old.

We did make a feeble attempt to stay away from each other, but found after we had both spent our lives in loveless marriages, we could no longer be Separated. Nigel insisted my name not be linked to his. He has paid an actress called Mary Jennings, who is preparing to retire to the country under another name, to put it about that it is she who is running away with him.

Perhaps you will think us selfish for wanting to be together. I shall not blame you if you do.

I have had the most awful Premonition I may never

see you again, Perry dear, and could not bear the thought of your not knowing the truth.

Please Forgive Me.

The letter was signed "Your Loving Mama."

The Marquess of Carrisworth sank down against the back of the sofa. He leaned his head back, covered his eyes with one hand, and allowed the missive to drop into his lap.

All the years since his mother left her family, he had believed her heartless and uncaring—a belief encouraged by his bitter father.

Memories from his childhood came to him. It was true he had often seen his mother weeping, but had been told by his father that women used tears to get their own way. He saw now that these convictions had hardened him, causing him to put up a shield between himself and the world.

A true picture of his family sprang into clear focus. Trapped in a loveless marriage with a man who tyrannized her, his mother had done her best, but had been miserable. While he would always regret not being close to her, it was comforting to know she too grieved the distance his father had demanded be put between them.

And his mother had loved him.

Poor Mama. Could he really blame her for grasping the one chance she thought she had at happiness, one that had, after all, ended in death when she'd run away with her true love, Verity's father?

Verity's father. Oh, dear God. Perry sat up on the sofa only to drop forward, his elbows resting on his knees, his head in his hands. How could he explain to Verity it was *his mother* that her father had run away with all those years ago? How would she react to the intelligence?

He remembered her work with the actresses and perceived how deeply wounded she was by her father's betrayal of his family. Knowing that it was his mother whom her father had loved, would Verity turn against him?

For a moment he toyed with the idea of not telling her. She need never know. But almost immediately he realized the foolishness of such a plan. Someday, although it was not likely, she might find out. Then, she would know he had deceived her—and Verity's high standards would forbid her from associating with him after such dishonesty.

His muscles tensed. No, he could not bear an estrangement between them.

The frozen barrier inside him had melted away with the gift of his mother's letter and the new understanding of his life and feelings. In its place was the sure knowledge that he loved Verity. There could be no secrets between them.

Lord Carrisworth remained where he was. He needed a few minutes to compose himself, then he would go and tell her the truth.

The ladies next door sat in the drawing room.

Downstairs before noon for the first time in memory, Lady Hyacinth was still excited about her conquest of Lord Killigrew at the Tremaines' ball. "I'm certain the gentleman will call on me this morning. I do hope he'll bring sweetmeats rather than flowers."

Lady Iris's mouth puckered, and she cast her sister a fulminating glare. She was sick to death of Hyacinth's boasting.

Verity stabbed a needle into a piece of stitchery deemed worthless by virtue of the fact its creator's mind was on a pair of teasing green eyes and a mouth that made her senses swim.

Lady Hyacinth patted her red curls. "Yes, any minute now we shall receive word of Lord Killigrew's arrival."

As if in answer to the statement, the double doors to the drawing room were thrown open and a wide-eyed Betty rushed inside. "Mrs. Barrington has gone!"

Verity's stitchery dropped to the floor as she rose to her feet in alarm. "What? Surely you mean gone out driving or shopping . . . ?"

Betty shook her head vehemently. "No, miss. I mean her bed ain't been slept in. And all her gowns are missin'. I found this letter addressed to you on the mantel in her room."

With a trembling hand Verity accepted the parchment and dismissed Betty. Unfolding the paper she began to read the contents out loud. "Dear Mouse, I am off on my travels again this time with a new husband—"

Verity broke off, her hand flying to her throat. Lady Hyacinth gasped, and Lady Iris thumped her cane on the floor. "Read on, gel! Don't keep us in suspense."

Verity swallowed hard and continued. "After Sir Ramsey left me so cruelly at the ball last night, a kind, older gentleman comforted me. We sat in a deserted room and came to know each other quite well. At length we decided that nothing would serve other than for us to fly to Gretna Green and be married at once. Afterward, we plan to travel to the continent. I expect I shall be away for a long time as he is most amorous. Goodbye, little sister. The next time I see you, Mouse, you will call me Lady Killigrew. Yours, etc."

A sharp cry sounded from Lady Hyacinth and she beat her fists on the settee cushion. "Monster! Philandering old roué! Arch-fiend!"

Lady Iris ignored the sounds of her sister sobbing into a large handkerchief and instead studied her shocked young friend. "Now, Verity, this is the best possible thing that could have happened to Louisa. You and I both know she was fast on the road to ruin. Indeed, I wonder just what went on in that deserted room with Lord Killigrew that forced this hasty marriage. But in any event, you may take comfort in the fact that his lordship has his title, forty thousand a year, and his estates are in good heart. Keep in mind that an older husband will be more tolerant of any diversions Louisa might indulge in."

Verity sighed and nodded. "I agree, my lady. It is just the suddenness of it all. Do comfort Lady Hyacinth. I believe I shall go to my rose garden. It is always a place where I can gather my thoughts."

Verity walked out of the room, and for once Lady Iris took pity on Lady Hyacinth. "Hush, Sister. 'Twas surely that his lordship believed he could not have you which forced him into Louisa's clutches."

Lady Hyacinth raised a tear-stained face. "Do you really think so, Iris?"

Lady Iris pulled her sister close and allowed her to cry on her shoulder. "Of course! Men were always such damn fools."

It was fortunate Lady Hyacinth could not see Lady Iris roll her eyes to the heavens.

Outside in the sunshine, Verity wandered through her rose garden, pausing here and there to examine a new bloom. Although she had been considerably shaken by the news of Louisa's elopement, she deemed Lady Iris's view of the situation straightforward. She must wish the best for Louisa and Lord Killigrew and go on with her own life.

Maybe her future would include the Marquess of Carrisworth.

Her gaze shifted from the deep red petals of a flower to the open door of her morning room. Inside, she could see his lordship sitting on the sofa, his head in his hands. Verity moved forward and stopped a few feet from the doorway, unobserved by him. She frowned, thinking he appeared troubled.

Then she saw the portrait placed beside a nearby chair. From her vantage point, Verity could see the likeness of the lady clearly. A wave of apprehension swept through her.

It was the woman of the miniature she had found in her father's room. She was sure of it. But no, she thought, shaking her head in confusion, how could that be? Verity's mind reeled.

She lifted the skirts of her pale pink morning gown and silently hurried back to Lady Iris's. She entered the house and dashed up the stairs to her room. Fumbling with the handle of the drawer where she had tossed the miniature to keep the ribbon away from Empress, Verity reached in and grasped the small portrait.

The woman's sad eyes stared back at her.

Totally baffled, Verity clutched the miniature in her hand and flew back down the stairs determined to confront the marquess. Voices in the drawing room prevented her from going out the back way. She pulled open the front door and, unmindful of her flustered appearance, quickly covered the distance between the two townhouses.

Digby opened the door to her, and Verity rushed past without a word to the startled butler. She burst into the morning room, surprising the marquess, who jumped to his feet. "Miss Pymbroke, what is wrong?"

Verity stood by the portrait holding the miniature in her hand and compared the two. Just as she had suspected, the two women were one and the same. She whirled around to face Lord Carrisworth. "Who is that lady?" she demanded.

He looked into the depths of her velvet brown eyes for a long moment. "My mother," he answered at last.

"Your mother," she cried incredulously. "What, pray tell me, was a miniature of your mother doing in my father's desk?"

Lord Carrisworth ran his hands through his hair. "Sit down, Miss Pymbroke. I was just going to call on you to reveal some astonishing facts I have learned only this morning."

Bewildered, Verity sat on the sofa and the marquess sat next to her. His eyebrows raised in a question, and after her nod, he removed the miniature from her cold hand and studied it for a moment.

When he looked at her again, Verity saw his green eyes held the same sad expression as the lady in the portrait. "I do not know how to begin, Miss Pymbroke, so I believe it will be best if you read this letter from my mother. The man doing the restoration work on the painting found it hidden behind the canvas."

Verity drew back. "My lord, I do not think it proper to read what can only be personal correspondence."

Lord Carrisworth thrust the parchment into her hands. "Devil take what is proper! 'Tis the only way you will understand."

Verity accepted the missive and began to read. Almost immediately her face whitened. "Oh, dear God," she whispered.

Fearing she might faint, Lord Carrisworth strode to the brandy decanter and poured a large measure of the liquid.

He returned to sit next to her, handing her the glass. "Here, stop for a moment and drink this."

Visibly trembling, Verity accepted the drink without her usual protests against strong spirits and took several sips. Placing the glass on a side table she continued to read while the marquess watched her carefully.

When she was done, she wordlessly handed back the letter and gazed at the roses outside the door. "My father did not run away with an actress, but with a lady of Quality. Someone he had loved in his youth—apparently never stopped loving. I tell you, my lord, I had long ago discerned the truth that Papa and Mama's marriage had been one of convenience. Naturally there can be no doubt now. This letter makes everything plain."

Lord Carrisworth reached to comfort her but she avoided his hands and rose to stand by the door to the garden. He followed her, positioning himself behind her and to one side.

"Miss Pymbroke—Verity, this has been a shock for both of us. But perhaps it is to the good that we have found out. For myself, I can better understand my mother and what she did and the effect it had on me. Can you not say the same regarding your father?"

Verity considered his words. "Yes," she replied slowly. "You have the right of it. Although I can never forget Mama's pain when Papa left. Nor can this knowledge erase the heartache of growing up without my father. But, I do comprehend their motivation. You know, it makes their deaths even more tragic."

"Yes," Lord Carrisworth replied seriously. He placed a hand lightly on her arm and turned her to face him. Her thickly lashed brown eyes were wet with unshed tears.

Verity stared into his green eyes. A tumble of confused thoughts and feelings assailed her. Desperately she

wanted him to kiss her the way he had at the Tremaines'
ball. She needed him to hold her in his strong arms, to
support her.

"Verity, my angel, this can have no bearing on *our*
relationship, on our feelings for each other," he told her.
His jaw tensed, and then he spoke haltingly. "I have
come to feel the greatest of affections for you."

Abandoning this rather ungraceful speech, Lord Carrisworth moved his hand to cradle the back of her head,
tilting her face up to his.

When Verity realized he was about to kiss her as she
was hoping he would moments before, she drew back.
He had not said he loved her. Besides, it would not have
made a difference if he had, she told herself firmly.
Society would be scandalized if the story of his mother
and her father ever got out. It was an ill-fated connection,
and ladies avoided being the subject of gossip at all costs.

She took a determined step away from the marquess.
"My lord, I must make it a rule that you not kiss me ever
again. Indeed, from this moment forward we shall revert
to our landlord and tenant relationship, and when that is
over we shall see each other only occasionally in public."

Surprise flashed across his lordship's features. "What
on earth are you talking about?"

"The revelations of your mother's letter mean we
simply cannot be associating with one another. It would
break every rule of genteel behavior and subject us to
unpleasant conjectures."

Lord Carrisworth stood very still and stared at her. "I
fail to see why. No one knows of any connection
between our families; you read what my mother wrote.
Hell and damnation, even I had no idea! And if my father
suspected it was your father Mother ran off with, he
never gave any indication. Since my father has been in

his grave these three years past, I think we can trust his continued silence."

Verity pursed her lips.

"Think, Verity!" the marquess snapped, fighting the need to shake some sense into her. "No one could possibly condemn any relationship between us."

Verity raised her chin stubbornly. "Even so, there would be undesirable talk. Give me your word you will not kiss me again."

The marquess threw his hands up in the air in a gesture of resignation. "Very well. I give you my word I shall not kiss you."

Perversely, hearing the words spoken aloud caused a rush of pain so intense Verity felt she would burst into tears right in front of him. Stiffly, she dropped him a brief curtsy, then rushed from the morning room, across the hall, and out the front door.

Perry stood with his fists clenched at his sides. His angry gaze remained fixed on the door through which Verity had exited.

How could he ever have dropped his guard enough to imagine himself in love with any woman, no less one with as many rules and moral strictures as Miss Verity Pymbroke? That she should cast aside his feelings in favor of her notion of some addlepated version of "genteel behavior." Famous!

Grim-faced, Lord Carrisworth picked up the brandy decanter. He strode to the library, whose door could only be said to be a credit to its maker since it did not fall to pieces under the strength of the slam it endured.

Outside on the street, a closed carriage was stopped across from Verity's townhouse. Pulling back the curtain, the occupant of the coach observed Verity's arrival and departure.

Roxanna hissed. The chit had appeared quite flustered both times. What was Perry doing with little Miss *Prim*broke?

Ever since the day a drunken Lord Carrisworth had brought Roxanna to the townhouse, she had been waiting for him to make her another offer of protection. No proposition had been made.

To make matters worse, her current benefactor, Rupert, the Duke of Covington, had learned of her presence with Carrisworth at Vauxhall and had given her her marching orders. Boldly, Roxanna planned to present herself on Perry's doorstep and use her charms to orchestrate her way back into her position as his mistress.

Tapping a long nail on the seat beside her, Roxanna decided her situation was desperate. Forgetting that Lord Carrisworth had dismissed her as his mistress long before he had met Verity, Roxanna viewed that Perry was too involved with the oh-so-innocent Miss Pymbroke to see he could have her, Roxanna, back in his bed.

And that meant Miss Pymbroke was an obstacle that would have to be removed once and for all.

Chapter Ten

Lady Iris was coming down the stairs from the drawing room where, with the aid of a fresh plate of pastries, she had finally succeeded in comforting Lady Hyacinth. She was startled when the front door swung open and a pale and shaking Verity hurried inside.

The older lady stopped on the bottom step. "Zounds! What the devil—"

Lady Iris broke off as Verity covered the distance between them, hurled herself into her arms, and burst into tears. Her ladyship reached up to keep her high white wig from flying off her head and then hugged her young friend. " 'Tis Carrisworth, I'll wager."

Verity sobbed harder.

"Come, gel. Let's go up to your room away from the eyes of the servants and you can tell me all about it." Lady Iris linked her arm with Verity's, and they climbed the stairs, her ladyship muttering under her breath the entire way. "I feared the handsome ass would do something stupid. He's led a rackety sort of life . . . not accustomed to dealing with a young miss of virtue . . ."

At last, they gained Verity's bedchamber. Lady Iris dipped a handkerchief into a bowl of cool water and then sat down on the bed next to the girl. She gently patted

Verity's tears away with the cloth and said, "What is this foolishness?"

The events of the morning tumbled from Verity's lips.

Lady Iris listened until the girl finished. Then she took a deep breath and asked, "Do you love Lord Carrisworth?"

Verity looked away from her ladyship's intelligent gaze. A moment passed before she whispered, "Yes. But it cannot signify."

Lady Iris scoffed at this reply. "His mother and your father running away together can mean nothing to your future with the marquess. And if you're thinking in terms of loyalty to your Mama, you're a fool. You were a good, devoted daughter, and I know she loved you. But I tell you where her husband was concerned she was a weak, silly thing who would never have been able to hold any man's interest."

Verity remembered how her mother had spent most of her life after the viscount's desertion lying on the morning room sofa, the epitome of the invalid. She had allowed her daughter to take over the running of the household as soon as Verity was old enough. Still, Verity deemed any deficiency on her mother's part not relevant to the present insupportable position she found herself in with the marquess.

Turning to face Lady Iris, she pursed her lips and then confided, "My lady, people might find out eventually about the undesirable connection and then the tale-bearers—"

Lady Iris let out an exasperated snort. "Cut line and give over, Verity. Society will *always* find someone to talk about. If one is the current subject of tittle-tattle, one simply holds one's head high and pays no attention."

Verity made as if to protest, but Lady Iris took both her hands in hers and squeezed them. "No, gel. You are being overly sensitive about what is proper. Idle gossip cannot matter. Unless I miss my guess, which I rarely do, Carrisworth is on the verge of offering for you. He will settle down—rakes make the best of husbands don't you know—and the two of you will rub along well together. *Don't* throw away a chance at happiness."

Mixed feelings overwhelmed Verity's thoughts. At length she blurted, "The marquess said he had a great affection for me. But he never said he loved me!"

"What! Of all the paper-skulled, beef-witted . . ." A martial light came into Lady Iris's eyes. "Well, that is really beyond all bearing! But Perry will realize his error and come to you. Mark my words. He's most likely suffering as much as you are right now—and it serves him right too. In the meantime you must regain your composure. Rest here for a while, gel."

Lady Iris helped Verity out of her gown and settled her into bed. "After the ball last night, we are bound to have callers this afternoon. I'll send Betty up in an hour to help you dress. You think on what I've said."

The older lady softly closed the door behind her, leaving Verity to her disordered thoughts. Was Lady Iris right? Did Lord Carrisworth want her as his wife? A sudden vision of his lordship's naked chest as she had seen it that day in the bath appeared in her mind's eye, and she experienced a rush of warmth. She relived the feelings his kiss had called forth at the Tremaines' ball and groaned.

She lay on the bed twisting and turning in her agitation. In this instance doing what was proper—terminating the intimate side of her relationship with Lord Carrisworth—had not brought about the usual feelings of gratification. Why?

Could it be that her feelings for his lordship were much more significant than her sense of what might be virtuous behavior? Was the real source of her pain that the marquess had not declared himself?

Lady Iris had not drawn the curtains around the bed. Out of the corner of her eye Verity caught a flash of golden light coming from her dressing table. She eased off the bed and crossed the room. The topaz eardrops the marquess had given her lay shimmering in the light.

Verity slowly picked them up, feeling a burning behind her eyes. Tears threatened but she held them back and walked over to her desk, pulling out a sheet of paper. The jewelry must be returned to the marquess at once.

If only she could ask him to return her heart.

Meanwhile, next door, the Marquess of Carrisworth was growing steadily drunk. Seated in the large leather chair behind the desk in his library, his lordship stripped off his coat, tossed it onto the floor, and reached yet again for the brandy decanter.

Mr. Wetherall watched the expensive garment crumple in an untidy heap and then glared at his master, his left eye twitching. "You allowed dear Miss Pymbroke to leave this house quite upset," he scolded. "I saw her from the upstairs landing."

Lord Carrisworth took a long drink of the liquid before turning a haughty eye on his valet. "You forget your place."

Mr. Wetherall's sparse frame stiffened. "And you choose to ignore yours. You should be on one knee in front of that sweet, pretty miss, asking for her hand instead of drowning your fears in drink."

"Fears!" The marquess rose angrily to his feet.

Mr. Wetherall did not give one inch. Staring straight at his employer, the valet's eye convulsed at the enormous lapse in the conventions he was making by confronting the young peer. However, the valet had rarely held his tongue when it came to serious matters. "Yes. You are afraid to tell her you love her. Afraid she'll *reject* you."

Lord Carrisworth opened his mouth prepared to give the impertinent old man a blistering set-down, devil take the number of years he had been in his service, when a scratching sound preceded the entrance of Digby. "The Earl of Northbridge has called, my lord."

"I am not at home."

The butler turned to leave, and Mr. Wetherall followed him out, but not before saying in a quiet voice that only just reached Lord Carrisworth's ears, "You mean you are not in your right mind. Mayhap the earl can set you straight. I'll send him in here directly."

Fortunately, Mr. Wetherall made it through the door before he could be subjected to a string of oaths that surely would have set his elderly ears aflame.

A moment later, the Earl of Northbridge entered the room. Taking in his friend's condition, he demanded an explanation. "Perry, what the devil is going on?"

"Just having a drink, Charles," he answered, returning to his chair. "Care to join me?"

The earl sat down across from him and studied his friend, deciding to tread slowly. "I accept. After all, I have something to celebrate. Cynthia and I found out this morning she is increasing. Excellent is smarter than that physician who told us no heir was on the way. Hah! She insisted we consult another doctor, and she was right."

Perry's mouth twisted in a parody of a smile. He poured Charles a brandy and passed it to him. "Congratulations," he drawled. " 'Twill be quite a sight to see you with some drooling brat hanging on to your sleeve."

Charles ignored the sarcasm. He could not remember ever seeing his friend so sunk in gloom. Several minutes of silence passed before Lord Northbridge spoke in a low voice, "Why don't you marry Miss Pymbroke, Perry? You shall not be happy until you do, you know."

The marquess's hand, in the act of reaching for another drink, stilled, and he stared into the earl's eyes. The genuine concern he saw there and the long years of their friendship forced him to pause before giving some cock-and-bull tale.

Good God, was it obvious to everyone he had formed a lasting passion for the chit? Perry rested his elbows on the smooth wood surface of the desk while he ran his hands through his dark hair.

At last he said, "I fear she would not have me, Charles." The minute the words left his tongue, Lord Carrisworth knew them to be the absolute truth. He wanted with Verity what Charles had with Cynthia. Nothing short of that would do, and that meant marriage.

Lord Northbridge leaned forward in his chair. "Did you ask her?"

"No."

A puzzled frown appeared between the earl's brows. "Then how can you know she would refuse you?"

Drawing in a deep breath, Lord Carrisworth outlined the morning's events ending with, "She values her notions of propriety more than me. Declared our relationship was nothing more than tenant and landlady."

The earl had given his total concentration to his friend's story. Now he sat rubbing his chin thoughtfully. "Perry, did you tell Miss Pymbroke you love her?"

Lord Carrisworth had the grace to look ashamed. "I only realized it myself this morning. Damme, Charles, I am so used to hiding my true feelings I stumbled over the words and instead spouted some blather about holding her in affection."

"Ah." Lord Northbridge nodded wisely. "That's it then, Perry. Females can be deucedly particular about hearing those words."

Lord Carrisworth considered his friend's suggestion. "Maybe you have the right of it, Charles."

The earl stood and leaned over to clap Perry on the shoulder. "Courage, old man . . . but, er, enough of the Dutch sort." He made to take his leave, eager to return to Cynthia, but at the door turned for a moment to inquire about a subject that had been perplexing him since his return to Town. "Perry, about the twins . . . did you ever . . ."

Lord Carrisworth waved a hand. "Do not be ridiculous, Charles. You cannot imagine a pair of more tiresome children."

Lord Northbridge let out his booming laugh and closed the door behind him.

After his friend's departure, Perry sat back in his chair and rubbed the back of his neck. He experienced a nagging anxiety that the proper Miss Pymbroke would cling resolutely to her convictions. But could Charles be right? Had he only to tell Verity he loved her? At the thought of her smiling on him and holding her arms out in welcome, the marquess felt all the tension drain out of him.

The library door opened, and Mr. Wetherall entered. He folded his arms across his chest expectantly and stared impudently at his employer.

"I require a pot of strong coffee and a hot bath to be brought to my bedchamber immediately," his lordship commanded.

The valet's wrinkled face broke into a grin.

* * *

Outside, Lord Davies sat in a closed carriage a short distance from Lady Iris's townhouse. He was biting his nails and mentally cursing Roxanna Hollings. He should have been on the road to Ramsgate by now before his creditors caught up with him. Why should he stoop to doing that whore's bidding?

Money. A mirthless laugh escaped his lips. That was why he had been waiting for some opportunity to present itself that would enable him to carry out Roxanna's latest plan.

The actress had come to his lodgings earlier in the day. "You poor dear man," she had cooed. "Everyone has quite turned against you since that unfortunate incident at Brook's. No doubt with an accusation of cheating at cards hanging over your head, not to mention the duns on your doorstep, you will find a sojourn to the continent beneficial."

The baron turned a cold eye on the actress. "State your business, madam. As you can see from the condition of these rooms, I am preparing for a journey. Ramsgate is a distance away, and I wish to quit London immediately."

Roxanna's lips curled. "You might find having a companion on the long trip advantageous."

Lord Davies's brows drew together. "What can you mean?"

Roxanna took a turn about the room before answering him. "Verity Pymbroke continues to be a hindrance to my wishes. I want you to ruin her once and for all. Take her with you as far as—Ramsgate was it? Then, before you board ship, simply desert her. She'll have been away overnight and be well and truly compromised. You will be long gone before she returns to London—if she manages to safely return—and will suffer no consequence.

On the contrary, a very large purse will add to your comfort during your exile."

Lord Davies appeared to consider this for a moment. "How do I know I will get my money?"

Roxanna shook her finger at the baron. "Tut. Tut. Don't you trust me? Well, as it turns out I don't trust you either. That is why my coachman will be driving you. He does not know the contents of the package he carries is money, only that he is to give it to you after your mission is completed."

Lord Davies's lips twisted. "Are you so desperate to have Carrisworth back in your bed? Is not the duke's protection enough for you?"

Roxanna had quickly looked away, and the baron had decided not to question her further. It was enough for him that he would be receiving a large sum of money for the small trouble of taking Miss Pymbroke along with him for part of his journey.

They had settled the details in a brisk, businesslike manner. All except one point. How was he to get the chit into the vehicle? She certainly was not going to come willingly after that scene at Vauxhall where he had kissed her in front of the marquess.

Lord Davies sat brooding over the possibilities, all the while thinking of the pistol that rested comfortably in the pocket of his lemon yellow coat.

Unaware of the danger that lurked outside, Verity welcomed Cynthia, Countess of Northbridge, into the drawing room. Lady Iris stayed only long enough to exchange pleasantries with the countess. She sensed that Verity might wish to confide in someone her own age and tactfully withdrew, leaving a sleepy Empress to climb into Verity's lap. Lady Hyacinth was abovestairs napping after the morning's ordeal of losing a beau to Louisa.

When Lady Iris left the room, Cynthia crossed to sit next to Verity on the blue satin settee. "I am so happy for this opportunity to be private with you, Verity," the countess said, her voice rich with excitement. "Charles and I called in another physician, and I am increasing after all."

Verity experienced a moment of sheer envy. What if she were married and found herself in the same interesting condition? Would the babe have Lord Carrisworth's green eyes or her brown?

Calling herself severely to task for such fanciful thoughts, Verity stroked Empress's soft silver fur. "I am so very happy for you and Charles, Cynthia. Truly the child will be blessed to have you and the earl as parents. I have never seen a couple more in love."

"Thank you," the countess responded, her face positively glowing. But, as Cynthia was ever sensitive to the feelings of others, she had noticed the slight puffiness around Verity's eyes.

Charles had come home and told her the events of the morning as related by Perry. Cynthia was determined to nudge Verity's thoughts to a more positive direction where the marquess was concerned without letting her know she was privy to their problems.

Therefore, the two chatted innocuously about the Tremaines' ball while munching on cakes and drinking tea until Cynthia rose to take her leave. "Verity, dearest, I hope you will not think me presumptuous—no," the countess interrupted herself, "I shan't care if you do think me so. I must tell you how delighted I was last night to see you and Perry together."

Standing next to Cynthia with Empress cradled in her

arms, Verity lowered her gaze to the ring of white fur on the top of Empress's head. She scratched the cat's ears bringing a purring sound into the quiet drawing room. "I am afraid being with the marquess in the intimate manner you found us was a mistake, Cynthia. There is no future for him and me."

The countess tilted her head in an inquiring manner. "Verity," she said gently, "be very sure before you come to such a conclusion. As one who has enjoyed all the wonders of a love-match, I beg you to consider your decision carefully. I know Perry has cultivated the reputation of a rake, but I also know him to be an honorable man."

"I see," Verity said noncommittally, and Cynthia picked up her reticule.

The two walked through the hall, the countess pensive. Finally, she chuckled and whispered, "For example, Verity, did you know that wicked man thoroughly enjoyed having the entire ton believe those two French girls were his mistresses."

Wide-eyed, Verity whispered back. "You mean, they really were not?"

Cynthia giggled. "No! In point of fact Perry only put them under his protection out of pity. It seems two elderly roués were after them. Oh, but my dear," the countess gasped, raising her gloved hand halfway to her lips, "Perry would be mortified if the truth got around. For some reason, he favors keeping people at a distance, and his reputation certainly accomplishes that."

"Yes," Verity replied faintly. A warm feeling infused her body at this latest bit of insight into Lord Carrisworth's character. This morning she had learned the reason why he had felt a need to keep people away so they could not hurt him.

They had reached the door, and Verity was brought out of her musings when Cynthia moaned. The countess pressed a hand to her stomach looking decidedly queasy.

Alarmed, Verity let Empress jump from her arms to the floor. She grasped Cynthia's arm. "Are you ill? Shall I take you abovestairs to rest?"

Cynthia's complexion had paled but she managed to smile ruefully. "No, it shall not be necessary, although I thank you for your kindness, dear. This discomfort most likely comes from my gluttony with your cook's delicious cakes. My carriage is right outside, and I shall do until I can get home."

Concern for Cynthia's condition made Verity step outside the townhouse and down the front steps. Despite the countess's protests, Verity walked her to her carriage and waited while the footman helped her into the coach before folding up the steps and taking his place on the back of the carriage.

Cynthia gave a weak smile and wave as the vehicle moved out into the line of traffic.

Watching the departing coach with a worried frown on her face, Verity never saw Lord Davies approach. But she did feel the cold steel of the pistol through her thin muslin gown.

"Walk," he commanded, indicating the direction by prodding her with the pistol.

Too shocked and frightened to do otherwise, Verity obeyed.

Empress, standing in the open doorway, saw the man with the tassels on his boots push Verity into a waiting carriage.

"Miaow!" she shrieked.

Entering the hall, Lady Hyacinth heard the fear in the

cat's voice, and her hands flew to her chest. "Merciful heavens, Empress—"

But she got no further as the cat raced out the door and down the front steps.

Lady Hyacinth followed her out the door where she saw the cat running down the sidewalk. "Empress! Come back here! Empress!"

Then with utter horror Lady Hyacinth saw where the cat was going. Verity was being forcibly bundled into a closed coach by Lord Davies—there was no mistaking his red hair.

With a lurch the coach pulled away from the curb and took off at a smart pace. The silver-gray cat raced after it and with an incredible flying leap landed in the empty tiger's perch, all eighteen claws holding on for dear life.

Chapter Eleven

The Marquess of Carrisworth felt refreshed and sober after his bath. He sat in the morning room sipping coffee and planning how he would approach Verity. Thinking to ask her to go with him for a turn around the Park as the day was fine, he had dressed for driving. He was confident he could persuade her to change her thinking even if he had to use his lips to do so.

Digby entered the room and extended a silver tray holding a missive.

Lord Carrisworth accepted the letter and dismissed the butler. When he opened the parchment, the topaz eardrops slipped from the paper onto his lap.

The marquess picked them up, remembering how they had gleamed in the moonlight the evening before against Verity's creamy skin. How they had sparkled like her brown eyes. How he had brushed them with his fingertips when his hand had moved around to cradle her head as he lowered his lips to hers.

He turned his attention to the brief message.

My Lord Carrisworth,

Thank you for lending me these, but I must return

them. As you know, I cannot keep such a gift as it would not be proper to do so.

Verity Pymbroke

Lord Carrisworth gritted his teeth and called himself every kind of fool. While he could not blame her for returning the jewels, as it truly was not done for a lady of genteel birth to accept such a valuable token, her refusal to keep them only served as a timely reminder that Miss Pymbroke would never abandon her strict principles.

Never.

"Digby!" he shouted, tossing the missive and the eardrops on a side table.

"Yes, my lord," the butler said, scurrying into the room.

"Have my curricle brought around at once." He would go for that ride in the Park alone. Maybe it would clear his head. It was the fashionable hour, and perhaps, the marquess thought quite miserably, he should consider the prospect of acquiring a new mistress instead of a wife.

Suddenly the door to the morning room burst open and Lady Iris stomped in, her wig askew. Lady Hyacinth trailed behind her using one of her shawls to wipe the tears that were streaming down her cheeks.

"Carrisworth! Verity's been kidnapped and they've got Empress, too!" Lady Iris barked out. "Hyacinth says that bloody miscreant Davies took her away in a closed carriage—"

"I did not say 'bloody,' " Lady Hyacinth declared hotly. "I never use oaths. So coarse. But Iris is wasting time, my lord. You must go after them. Now. You gentlemen know how to go about these things." Lady Hyacinth made a shooing motion as if to hasten the marquess on his way.

Perry stood very still, his fists clenched at his sides. His cool and determined tone belied the wave of sheer black fright that had taken over every fiber of his being. "Naturally, I shall go after her. But I must understand exactly what happened so I may determine how best to proceed." He turned a burning green gaze toward Lady Iris, knowing she would be the more coherent.

Lady Iris reached up and straightened her wig. "Perhaps half an hour past Bingwood found Hyacinth in a swoon out on the front steps. He got her inside and summoned me. Took forever to bring her around and get the story out of her. It seems Hyacinth was crossing the hall when her attention was caught by Empress. The cat was standing in the open doorway to the front entrance raising the devil of a ruckus. When Hyacinth went to investigate, Empress took off down the street."

Lady Hyacinth could remain silent no longer. "That is when I saw Lord Davies *pushing* Verity into a *closed* coach. And she was without her gloves or bonnet!"

"I'm sure had she known she was about to be kidnapped she would have gotten the damn gloves and bonnet beforehand!" Lady Iris yelled at her sister.

Lady Hyacinth erupted into fresh tears.

"Ladies!" the marquess roared, his control snapping. A half hour ago! Good God, the dastard could have taken her anywhere in that time. Thinking aloud he said, "Davies was recently disgraced at the gaming tables. Although I fail to see what that would have to do with Miss Pymbroke. Despite certain events at Vauxhall I cannot believe he has formed a violent *tendre* for her which would lead him to whisk her away to Gretna Green."

"Verity's got no money so he couldn't be thinking of compromising her to get his hands on a large dowry,"

Lady Iris pointed out. "By Jupiter, I have always thought there was something doubtful about him besides the fact he fancies himself a Dandy. Heard he divides his time between his tailor, the gaming tables, and the theater."

"Yes, that's right," Lady Hyacinth put in eagerly, her tears stopping abruptly. "Why, I was taking tea with Lady Edwina the other day, you know she has the *best* French cook, and between the most delicious scones she told me Lord Davies was often seen in the company of that actress, my lord, the one you used to . . . oh, dear, that is, I mean to say . . ."

Lord Carrisworth sharpened his gaze on Lady Hyacinth. "Do you mean Roxanna Hollings?"

Lady Hyacinth nodded her head, clearly embarrassed at having referred to his lordship's former mistress.

The marquess's thoughts raced. Roxanna. Could she have something to do with this? He knew the actress wanted to be his mistress again. With London gossip being what it was, she was most likely aware of his interest in Verity. But why would she be desperate enough to—with a sickening feeling in his stomach Lord Carrisworth realized word in the clubs was that the Duke of Covington had severed his connection with Roxanna. She was currently without a protector, a situation that might very well make a grasping woman reckless. He must find out what she knew about Verity's abduction.

"Well," Lady Iris fretted, "do you think you can find her?"

"I shall not rest until I do," Lord Carrisworth informed her.

All three went out into the hall, the marquess picking up his hat and driving gloves from a table. "Digby!" he called.

When the harried butler materialized and assured his

lordship his curricle was waiting for him outside, the marquess turned toward the ladies. "Go home and await word from me there."

Lady Iris reached out to touch his sleeve. "And Empress, you won't forget her, will you? Hyacinth said the brave thing ran after the carriage and clung to it as it pulled away."

"No, ma'am, I shall not neglect to bring the little one home," his lordship assured her, managing a tight smile.

Then he was gone, leaving the ladies standing close together.

Roxanna was lounging in bed seemingly without a care in the world when the Marquess of Carrisworth crashed open the door to the room.

"Perry, my darling!" she exclaimed, scrambling out of the bed to hurry to his side. She stopped a few feet away when she saw the seething anger that hardened his features.

"Where has he taken her?" the marquess bit out.

Roxanna's face was the picture of innocence. "Whatever are you speaking of—"

Lord Carrisworth took a step toward his former mistress. His angry gaze swung over her, and he allowed her to see the contempt with which he held her. "Tell me without the tiniest bit of delay, Roxanna."

She sputtered, then, realizing the game was over, tried one last tactic. "Ramsgate. The baron is leaving the country and confided in me he was going to take Miss Pymbroke with him. I believed she truly wanted to go, Perry. Some women like a strong man—"

Lord Carrisworth cut her off, his voice cold and lashing. "Be silent! Davies does not care for Miss Pymbroke nor she for him. You must have offered to pay him and the baron, because he has been ostracized from Society and is probably the only man in London who has not heard you are no longer with Covington and therefore not in a position to obtain funds. Although why you thought that ruining the woman I love might benefit you I am blessed if I know. Nothing could have ever induced me to entangle myself with you again."

Roxanna's expression became defiant and her face flushed an unbecoming red.

The marquess turned on his heel without another word and quit the room. As he rushed down the stairs, he could hear Roxanna's scream of pure fury.

It was hard to tell if Verity or Lord Davies was more miserable inside the traveling coach.

They had been on the road without a break for close on two hours. Verity's initial fear had dissipated and been replaced by anger and determination. She felt confident she could get away from the useless fop sitting across from her if only the carriage would stop bowling over the countryside.

Indeed, she fumed, she had behaved stupidly by allowing Lord Davies to bully her into the coach in the first place. While she remained totally baffled as to why he had kidnapped her since he refused to tell her anything but that they were for Ramsgate, she did not believe for a moment that he was capable of pulling the trigger of the pistol he held on her.

Her chief concern was how to get back to London once away from her captors. She knew from Lord Davies that the coachman was part of the scheme, so trying to persuade him to help her would net her nothing.

Verity rested her head on the back of the seat and wondered if Lord Carrisworth was aware of her disappearance. Would he find it ironic that she had seemingly fled to Ramsgate with another man? Her heart jumped when she realized he most likely had no idea where she had gone. How could he? Dear God, what if she never saw him again? Verity felt panic rise in her chest and forced herself to take a deep breath.

She pushed thoughts of the marquess from her mind. What of Lady Iris and Lady Hyacinth? They would be frantic when they discovered her missing.

Verity glared at Lord Davies. "Pray, when are we going to stop? I have suffered enough with this constant bouncing and jostling. Could you not have at least been considerate enough to hire a well-sprung vehicle for the gross impropriety of this journey that you have foisted on me?"

Instead of answering, Lord Davies shot her a look of loathing and wished Verity Pymbroke at the devil. He had been subjected to her moralizing for the better part of an hour. He was tired, thirsty, hungry, and his hand holding the pistol on his victim felt cramped. Worst of all, his cravat, normally a source of pride, was wilting.

He had been seriously considering ordering the coachman to hand over the package he was to deliver at Ramsgate now and set off on his own. "We shall break at the next inn for refreshments."

Verity tried to keep the excitement from showing on her face. This was it! She would simply excuse herself to take care of a personal need and then run.

What she had not counted on was the burly coachman who pulled out his own pistol when Lord Davies stepped into the Russell Arms Inn to procure food and drink. Nor had she realized twilight was upon them and, even if she did get away, she would have to find her way back to

London alone in the dark. Anxiety threatened to overwhelm her and she swallowed hard.

Still, she thought, climbing down from the coach, it might be the only chance she would have. "Excuse me, but I shall just step around back for a moment," she told the coachman firmly.

"I'll go with yer." The man's leering grin revealed several missing teeth.

Bother! Verity felt tears of frustration form behind her eyes. The frightening thought that she had underestimated the baron ran through her mind and she shivered.

To one side of the small inn was an ill-kept garden with a few tables and chairs set about. Lord Davies reappeared from inside the inn and motioned them to a table.

Verity bit her lip as the coachman led her to a seat next to the baron, then took up a position a short distance away, still leering at her.

A serving girl brought out a tankard of ale for Lord Davies and some wine for Verity. Thick slices of bread and cheese and a plate of blackberry tarts were set before them. Verity's stomach let out an unladylike rumble, but she was too nervous to eat.

Suddenly, from out of nowhere, Empress jumped up onto the table, rapidly traversed the few steps to Lord Davies's tankard of ale, lowered her head, and began to drink thirstily, spraying drops of ale in her exuberance. Her long silver fur was matted and small pieces of grass and straw clung to her from her long ride on the tiger's seat.

"Empress!" Verity cried in astonishment.

Lord Davies rose to his feet. "Hey! That blasted cat! How the devil did it get here?"

Empress paused in her drinking to stare at the baron with catly disdain. Then she casually hopped off the table and began inspecting Lord Davies's Hessian boots. More specifically, the tassels that decorated them.

The baron's face turned purple. "Oh no, you will not, you vicious defiler of boots!" So caught up was he in his rage at the cat for her previous offense, which he viewed was about to be repeated momentarily, that he forgot his surroundings and his circumstances and pointed his pistol at the feline.

Verity watched in horror as he took aim at Empress. "Stop!" she screamed, then lunged at his arm which was holding the deadly pistol, causing it to swing wildly to the left. The gun went off, and the company heard a bloodcurdling howl from the coachman who clutched his leg and fell to the ground. The innkeeper and several patrons came running.

A curricle sped into the midst of the calamity; it halted in the yard and its driver sprinted to the scene.

"Perry!" Verity cried and threw herself into his arms.

Lord Carrisworth held her tightly for a moment, then pulled her away a bit to gaze anxiously into her brown eyes. "You are not hurt?"

"No, my love, I am not. But how ever did you find me?"

Relief surged through the marquess at finding Verity safe. A relief that was heightened by hearing the words "my love." He raised a hand to smooth a wayward curl from her cheek. "Go inside the inn. Allow me to take care of some business here, and then I shall drive you back to Town."

The innkeeper's wife, recognizing members of the Quality and shooting her husband a dark look for having not done so earlier, fussed over Verity while leading her inside where she could freshen up.

But Verity was impatient to be with the marquess and

took but a few moments to wash her face and hands before she was back downstairs.

Lord Carrisworth was waiting for her and smiled at her entrance. "Come, my avenging angel, I shall explain all to you on the drive. We must be on our way. As it is, darkness has fallen, and I fear for your reputation."

"We cannot forget Empress," Verity breathed, hardly able to keep from staring into his eyes.

The marquess chuckled. "She seems a bit bosky and is already asleep in the middle of the curricle seat. I shall allow you to move her to the floor."

Once they were on their way, with a disgruntled Empress at their feet, Lord Carrisworth explained Roxanna's plan. He told Verity how he had pushed his horses to their limits in order to catch up, fearing he would not be able to do so.

He neglected to tell her of the facer he had planted on the baron's left jaw. "Lord Davies was quite upset upon finding the package that was supposed to be filled with money contained plain paper. He is for the continent, though, and we shall not be troubled by him. As for Roxanna, I shall see to it that no gentleman, er, finds an interest in her again."

Verity huddled closer to him on the curricle seat. She did not want to dwell on Roxanna and Lord Davies. There was something she had to say to Lord Carrisworth. Something she had come to realize during the afternoon's events. Her heart thumped in her chest. Clearing her throat, she opened her mouth to speak, but he put an arm around her and said, "Try to rest, my landlady."

The tension and strain caught up to her, and Verity leaned her head against his shoulder and closed her eyes.

When next she opened them, she saw they were

driving through the Mayfair streets. Verity sat up and adjusted her skirt.

"Are you feeling better?" the marquess inquired as he pulled his team to a stop at the curb in South Audley Street. He made as if to get down, but she stayed him by placing a hand tentatively on his arm.

Once she had his attention, Verity glanced away nervously. What if he did not want her after all? "My lord, I have been thinking, and I have come to the conclusion . . . well, it makes no difference to me what our parents did or if Society discovers their secret."

He remained silent, and Verity looked up to see him gazing at her with an expression so filled with love it quite took her breath away. Pulled by her own passion, she leaned closer to him and placed a hand on his cheek.

The Marquess of Carrisworth's voice was ragged. "I have given you my promise that I would not kiss you."

"Break it," Miss Verity Pymbroke commanded.

His lordship was more than happy to oblige her, holding her in his arms and lowering his lips to hers in a kiss that left no question as to his feelings for her.

After a few drugging minutes, he set her away from him. His deep voice teased her. "Really, Miss Pymbroke, this public display of affection will make us a subject for the lampoons. Why I see fat old Lord Mumblethorpe raising his quizzing glass at us from across the street."

"I care not a snap of my fingers," Verity declared. She proved this point by placing a hand around the marquess's neck and allowing him to kiss her again.

When he could not take any more, Lord Carrisworth raised his head and looked deeply into her eyes. "I love you, Verity, with all my heart. The rules of proper behavior for a gentleman state that he is to drop to one knee when he asks a lady to marry him, but since we are in this cursed curricle with a cat at our feet . . ."

Verity's face broke into an expression of pure joy. "Oh, Perry, I do love you so. There is nothing I want more than to be your wife."

The couple embraced yet again, oblivious to the feline who jumped out of the curricle and ran a bit unsteadily up the steps, to Lady Iris's townhouse. "Miaow!" she cried, bringing Lady Iris and Lady Hyacinth to the door. The two older ladies looked beyond the cat at the couple locked in each other's arms in the curricle.

Lady Hyacinth whispered, "Well, Iris, did I not tell you they would get together?"

Lady Iris glared at her sister. "You? It was my plan for him to rent her townhouse that brought them together."

"Do not be silly, Iris. That was the merest coincidence and you know it."

Lady Iris scowled and looked down at her pet.

Empress dropped one eyelid in an unmistakable wink. Then she let out a delicate hiccough.

Next door, Mr. Wetherall was passing by a window and chanced to look outside and see his master and Miss Pymbroke. He dropped the entire stack of newly starched cravats he was carrying and performed a mad jig.

Down in the street, Verity was saying, "Perry, I must make it a rule that you kiss me that way every day of our lives."

The marquess smiled at his love. "You know, my sweet landlady, that is one rule I daresay I shall follow."